P9-EDW-726

TW

FROM MY FATHER, SINGING

FROM
MY
FATHER,
SINGING

a novel by

DAVID BOSWORTH

PUSHCART

PUBLISHER'S NOTE

This novel is a work of fiction. Names, characters, places, and incidents are either the product of the author's imagination or are used fictitiously, and any resemblance to actual persons, living or dead, events, or locales is entirely coincidental.

Winner of the 1986 Editors' Book Award

Sponsoring editors for the Editors' Book Award are Simon Michael Bessie, James Charlton, Peter Davison, Jonathan Galassi, David Godine, Daniel Halpern, James Laughlin, Seymour Lawrence, Starling Lawrence, Robie Macauley, Joyce Carol Oates, Nan A. Talese, Faith Sale, Ted Solotaroff, Pat Strachan, Thomas Wallace. Nominating editor for this novel: Natalie Greenberg.

ISBN 0-916366-36-7
LC 85-060720

Manufactured in the United States of America by RAY FREIMAN AND COMPANY

PUBLISHED BY PUSHCART PRESS
P.O. BOX 380, WAINSCOTT, N.Y. 11975

to
Alex and Gabe,
to
Mom and Dad
—from the one between

FROM MY FATHER, SINGING

Chapman's Yankee Trader, Rte. 45. Gas. Foodstuffs. Sandwiches. Drugstore products (hair spray, toothpaste, band-aids) without a pharmacist. Local papers in the front, beneath a row of paperback books which are gathering dust. No *Times*, no *Globes*: they went south, with the tourists and the geese, late last month. Hatchet blades? kerosene? — try aisle six. Dry goods, ma'am? — aisle three, toward the rear, just across from the fishing gear. We have it all there: workshirts, clothespins, no-nonsense under-wear; everything the sensible man could want or need. Everything for a price.

Chapman's Yankee Trader, Rte. 45. Outside, an hour after dawn, the cool September sun is slow to burn off a soaking fog. The mountains, scrufty and sparse, scarcely more than hills, stretch off to the left, their flanks obscured by skirts of mist. A semi lumbers by, rattling the storefront glass, carrying produce to Chapman's competitor, an IGA twenty miles to the west. Drawn, I turn from the register to watch it pass: my life is now measured by "events" like this.

In Jersey now, in Colton Falls, six hundred miles and

two months to the south, the citizens would just be rising from their beds, their morning rituals acted out by rote while still half-asleep. An electric razor; a silky tie picked from a rack in the closet; one muffin, well-done, with strawberry jam; a briefcase by the door beneath the burglar alarm. According to script, Marjorie would murmur, her sleepy voice muffled by a quilted comforter, "Have a good day, Dear." According to script, Robbie would lie, doe-eyed and trusting, awake in his crib, waiting for me and my goodbye kiss. Six hundred miles to the north, all is still. The truck gone, I can just barely hear, as if the rush of my own blood within my ears, the perpetual perpetual hum of the mill. At the rear of the store, a loose board creaks (the floors are planked like a boardwalk here but, spared the weather, are smoother to the feet). It is Chapman, I know, checking to make sure that I've repriced the canned beans.

It's a Friday, 7:30 a.m. Four mill hands, released from the night shift, have arrived together in their pickups and drifted in. Vaguely middle-aged, they wear bargain boots and workshirts, blue or green chinos faded from washings and smelling of sawdust. To an outsider, to me, they look very much alike, but of course they're not. And the Yankee Trader serves them all, whatever they're like. Be they Methodist, Congregationalist, Baptist, or Catholic, be they drinkers or abstainers, be they Republican or Democrat; he'll even sell to an atheist or someone on food stamps — to any man or woman in Johnson Mills, Maine. The "democracy of commerce" which has made America great.

And he sells it all. The Trader is not *in* or *at* but *equal to* the center of town. Here the townsmen buy their food, their gas, cash their checks; out back, used furniture and boats for rent. Chapman has a tow truck if they need one and will call himself a mechanic if you're an out-of-towner and willing to believe it. Everything for a price.

The beans, for example, cost forty-five cents — up two from just last week. He'll check them all, Chapman will, the loose floorboard creaking beneath the repetitious weight of his scrutiny, to be absolutely sure that I've marked them right. "A lost cent is a lost chance" is his favorite expression, the aphoristic lecture with which he chastizes his children (is that how Marjorie's father made his million?): *a lost cent is a lost chance.* And you might as well substitute "soul" for "chance" so grave and theological is the cast to his voice. The children, a son and two daughters, my fellow workers, look so much like him that one is led to wonder if they have a mother — red-haired, thin, with wide foreheads and narrow chins and dark green eyes which rarely blink. The only employee not born to him, I've learned to take my cues from them, the cautious quiet Chapman kids. Like them, I never interrupt their father when he talks; like them, if with a bit more irony than awe, I refer to him as "Mr. Bob." That's *MISS-tah Baahb.*

As a father Mr. Bob is hard but fair. He is the sort of disciplinarian who never has to raise his voice or lift a hand. Contrary to the cliché, he can be positively chatty in a slow-paced way, but if you're a stranger, he'd just as soon lend you money as carry on a conversation. "Minimum wage" were the first two words I heard from him, and that was all he had to say while I clumsily tried to explain myself and why I was there — a thirty-five year old, six hundred miles away from home, applying for a job at minimum wage. He didn't want to hear. Even the most general description of my situation, with its rancid air of domestic disaster, smacked too much of a confession to him and a violation, therefore, of *his* privacy — his right not to know. Offended, he stared straight through me until, out of desperation and fear of his silence, I mentioned that my father had been born two towns to the north, in Little Chester.

I could see at once that it made a difference. His eyes squinted, narrowing with such sudden interest and intensity that he might have been reading the day's receipts from the Yankee Trader's register. "Little Chester," he said, his eyes releasing me at last, and then, exasperated, shook his head as if to add: "Why, in God's name, didn't you say so in the first place?"

Here, in Johnson Mills, genealogy and geography are the only relevant recommendations.

Their shopping finished, the mill hands have gathered now in the open space before my register. It's Friday, pay day, and they're louder than usual, laughing, dawdling a bit, taking time to razz each other and smoke an extra cigarette, in a semi-conscious way proud of themselves: they've survived another week, they've done their man's work without complaint, they've provided for their families and have their proof in the Northern Timber paychecks they carry in their hands. And yet the amounts are so small that their pride seems a joke, played on them; so apparently insufficient that I'm frightened for them, wondering how they'll survive the winter. It's Mr. Bob's inflexible rule, a matter of Yankee Trader principle, that for a check to be cashed something in turn, no matter how small, must be bought from the store, so every Friday these men come in from the mill to buy candy for their wives, women whose thighs have already ballooned from too many children and carbohydrates. All-day suckers; gum drops; bite-sized chocolates — the only "sweet life" they'll ever savor. (Many are toothless.) Valentines from loyal husbands.

14

In Jersey now, Colton Falls, gardeners would be busy on their clients' lawns, school buses beginning to make their rounds, garage doors opening by remote control — drawbridges to macadam moats. A black maid or two would be walking in from the bus stops, about to clean house for someone else, answer the phone and prepare the dinner; about to play parent to another's children. Outside, at 7:35, the fog has thinned, gas being pumped by a Chapman kid, Robbie still waiting in his crib for my goodbye kiss; the mill hands have started laughing again — at a joke I overhear but don't understand.

Turning, I see that they've paused to listen to Calvin Wynn. An old-timer with finger joints like petrified wood, he arrives here at every change in shift, plants himself near the register where he can assault a captive audience with his repetitious stories about the mill. "We worked those splitters day and night," he says, his neck outstretched, his eyes owl-wide (he's lived here, it's plain to see, all his life): *"day — and — night!"* His stare is a dare, but no one is going to deny what he's said. Instead, pretending to be impressed, listening with a mix of respect, amusement, tolerance — maybe even fear (do they see themselves like this in forty years?) — they include him for the moment in their celebration. But when they turn to me their expressions change; cautious nods, averted eyes, a perfunctory *"Morning"* just to let me know they're not impolite. This is as far as I've come. And if I live here twenty years instead of two months, I begin to doubt that I'll ever get past this stiff-arming courtesy which is at heart both a form of suspicion and a self-defense.

The last purchase nears, a package of licorice for twenty-five cents. I imagine Mr. Bob smiling inside at the rear of the store as he hears the ring of the register: he's a

15

quarter richer, less expenses — twenty-five chances he didn't miss. The customer, I've seen before. He's around my age and always wears a baseball-style cap with "Rockwell Speedway" stamped on the front. Like me, he is over six feet tall and has thick-rimmed glasses, although his, I notice now, as if bug-struck windshields, are speckled with sawdust. If my father hadn't moved away after school, if he had stayed, somehow met my mother anyway and I had been born, would this mill hand and I have been teenage friends, shared cars and beers, surreptitious cigarettes in the cafeteria, raised hell together at the regional high? Would I, too, now be wearing a cap with "Rockwell Speedway" stamped on the front, my vision of male glory, instead of center court at the U.S. Open, a beauty queen's kiss on my sooty cheek for being first to cross the finish line? A hundred-and-forty-three fifty, minus a quarter — on this, he'll have to support himself, his wife, his sons and daughters. (*How will he do it?*) As I count out the bills, remembering that the gardeners in Colton Falls wanted nearly that much for merely tending to a lawn five times a month, our hands in the exchange accidentally brush; as if shocked, we both automatically recoil from the touch. My life is now measured by "events" like this.

Quickly he slips away. Past the papers, past the dusty books, across the worn wooden floor, my might-have-been friend makes his escape; heads for the open front door where his fellow workers wait. There, they laugh again; laugh not about me but without me — I can't join in. I've lost the right; I'm forbidden their relief, their sense of celebration at the end of the week, their justified pride. I don't belong with them, these fathers, these providers, these natives of the land, and their laughter, carried back to

16

me now by the cool damp air, sinks in with a chill, bringing a sudden fear as I hear their engines rev and their truck doors slam, that I will die alone in Johnson Mills, two towns south of where my father was born — alone and damned.

Chapman's Yankee Trader, Rte. 45. I am in exile here, on the lam. From memos and garden hose, from scripted mornings and fathers-in-law. I have done the unforgivable.

I have left my boy behind.

1.

Dear Son, dear Robbie, my son: You won't be able to understand this now, but I'm hoping that in a few years, when you've seen a bit more of the world as it is, I'm hoping that then you'll begin to feel . . . Dear son, dear Robbie, my son: I know it's too soon for you to forgive what I've done, I know that you feel that I've let you down, but . . . but if . . . but if you could just . . . Dear Son: To be honest, Rob, I'm beginning to doubt that I can pull this off. There's too much confusion, despair, self-disgust; too many settings (three), too many fathers (four at least), too many sins to rationalize. And the fog is slow to burn off in my mind.

In the Department of the Housing Inspector, the city of Trenton, the place where I pretended to earn our living — a living which, I am ashamed to admit, was increasingly subsidized by your mother's trust fund interest and other subversive incarnations of your grandfather's "gifts" — there was a joke sign sitting on the Chief Inspector's desk, and that joke sign said: PLAN AHEa$_d$.

The message was self-mocking, the desk a paper-littered advertisement for procrastination. A husband of the

19

mayor's cousin, the Inspector was a pleasant, lazy, bewildered man whose incompetence was offset by an irrepressible cowlick, a boyish expression, and that aura of gentleness which failure can sometimes bring to people who refuse to take refuge in bitterness. I liked him and he liked me, in part because I ran the department for him, because I was willing to shoulder without complaint his official responsibilities. It was a tacit arrangement, this transfer of command. At the end of our long lunches together, lunches extended by his garrulousness, he would simply hand over, without a word of instruction or acknowledgment, those incoming memos which had been rained down on him by members of the administration more ambitious than he. Memos on hiring procedure, memos on charity contributions, memos on office supplies and retirement parties — memos I would spend the afternoon disposing of. (Pay attention, Rob: this is just the sort of bullshit you're likely to face when you grow up.) There was even a memo on memos one memorable day. "Memo. Subject: Memos," it said. "A memo should be succinct, well-reasoned, easily read. Always organize your thoughts before you begin. Use an outline format whenever you can." . . .

. . . An outline, then. *(PLAN AHEa$_{d.}$)* My thoughts organized before I begin.

       I. Memo to Myself

          A. Subject: A Letter to My Son, Robert Douglas, Age One Year, Nine Months

             1. Explain Letter
             2. Explain Self — apologize

20

3. Explain Wife (careful here)
4. Explain World (God? sex? money? death?)
   — tips, advice, etc.
5. Conclusion (in an upbeat mood; as reassuring as possible)
   — "I will always love you even though . . ."

Dear Son: Before I move ahead, before I attempt to address God, sex, your mother, and death, I have to turn back to correct an impression I've made, because even though I still doubt that I can pull this off, even though I'm more sure with each passing word that this will not be succinct, well-reasoned, or easily read, I know that if my letter is to work at all it will have to be an honest one. And honesty demands a more balanced view of those lunches I had with the Chief Inspector; it requires that I reveal to you a less flattering aspect of our tacit arrangement.

We ate in. So complete were his laziness and resignation, so profound his sense of physical inertia, that not even lunch could beckon the Inspector away from the soft rocking chair behind his desk. Sandwiches would be sent up. I would arrive a few minutes late. The door would be closed, the phone put on hold, the day suspended for an hour or so while we devoured together our disagreeable food, picnicking atop his all-purpose desk. (Whenever I consider my present situation, all the messiness and confusion, the lack of resolution, I can't help but envision that lunchtime desk: its unruly explosion of memos, folders, citation forms, and messages; our sandwich wrappers resting on top, beside styrofoam cups sprouting soggy straws and napkins bloodied with tomato sauce; that sign, that cartoon caption, peeking out from the rubble like an air-raid victim — PLAN AHEa_{d.)}

He loved to talk, the Chief Inspector did. As with most men who are immune to success, he loved to speculate and reminisce, forever removing himself from the present tense where there was the risk of real accomplishment. The subject of these midday ramblings, interrupted by bites into sausage subs and tuna salad sandwiches, was always the same. No matter where he began, the thread would inevitably meander back to our mutual boss, that cousin of his wife, a man whose venality and craftiness, whose vindictiveness and audacity, if one were to believe the Inspector's stories, had never been matched in even New Jersey's byzantine past of civic malfeasance and mismanagement. The Mayor's tax maneuvers, his derring-do escapes from prosecution, his manipulation of the press, his insatiable appetite for bimbo secretaries and subordinates' wives; where the kickbacks went, which city contracts were fixed, how homes were owned on the Florida coast in the name of distant relatives — the accounts went on and on until their subject began to assume a life of its own, an existence above and beyond the short and balding immigrant's son who shook my hand every Christmastime. Something legendary and fantastic, something half absurd and half heroic. A yeti of graft. A Paul Bunyan of political corruption.

There was an ambiguous aura of both disapproval and awe to those long lunchtime monologues. I didn't doubt that the Inspector, as he so often insisted, was genuinely offended by the larcenous character of this in-law who had appointed him. And yet he so lived in the Mayor's shadow, he was so dependent on the man, not only for his job but for the very content of his thoughts, the very image against which he defined himself, he so relied on him as the living excuse for his own irredeemable incompetence (in this man's world, his stories were always designed to imply, only bastards like the Mayor could be successful), that it was impossible to imagine him except as some kind of append-age — an extra finger, say, or feckless appendix — to the corpus of myth which he had spun about the Mayor's existence. It was a relationship I had seen before, the submergence of the vassal within the life of the lord. The Inspector's fixation, which even at its most resentful was a secret form of admiration, reminded me of the way soldiers speak about their toughest C.O.s or students about their strictest principals. It reminded me, Rob, I'm sorry to say, a connection I repressed until it was too late, of the way your mother used to speak about her father.

Our lunchtime script, like my early morning script, like every daily scene, it began to seem, in my life back then, rarely changed. The Inspector would talk. I would lean back in my chair, pick at my lunch, refuse to interrupt, practicing a sort of patience then, born in part of conde-scension, which is so unlike the patience I'm learning now while stationed behind the register, waiting, always waiting for the next event, for a passing truck, for a change in shift, a story retold by Calvin Wynn, watching the moon eclipsed by the hem of a fir as I rock on the porch of the cabin I rent. Yes, my patience was condescending then. I indulged the Inspector and his dubious accounts of the Mayor's dealings, but it's important to understand that he indulged me, too, that he was just as patient with *my* weaknesses.

For certain memos were not included in those piles he handed over at the end of each lunch; certain orders were not passed on, diverted instead to other hands. The Inspector, it seems, was my self-appointed censor. Alert to which instructions would offend my rarified version of civic ethics, he was careful to shield me from the use of our department as a political weapon, sparing me the harrassing inspections, the "lost" citations, the demeaning quest for contributions from the very businesses we were supposed to police. I was "cherry," you see. (You'll have to wait awhile, Rob, to understand fully what that metaphor means.) I was what the Mayor's political men — an unattractive mix of old ward heelers, fat with graft, and New Age consultants, weaned on soap ads and oiled with an easy cynicism — called "cherry," a good-government type who liked to pretend that the city could be run on the Ten Commandments. That such false innocence could continue to exist in the very midst of the Mayor's foul nest was a direct result of the Inspector's efforts. It was in a way his *quid pro quo*, the less flattering aspect of our tacit arrangement. He protected my favorite lie because I protected his. I allowed him to pretend that he was in command, and he, in turn, allowed me to pretend that ours was a cherry operation. And all this collusion, this improvised marriage of our self-delusions, was enacted without a word being said.

It's amazing, Rob, what a man can pretend. Fantasy is supposed to be the province of children and yet every adult I know re-imagines the world to better fit his expectations; every man I've met lies to himself about his condition. It seems, I'm sorry to conclude and so much sorrier to have to report it to you, that people are not very happy with life as it is. The Inspector needed to pretend that he was in command. I needed to pretend that our department was clean. My mother needed to pretend for thirty years that my

24

father's lack of ambition was temporary. Your mother needs to pretend that the money she accepts is merely "lent," that she is free of her father's influence. She needs to pretend that she has not changed, that despite her trust fund, her broker, her house in the suburbs — these, she is quick to explain, were acquired for your sake (Please forgive us, Son, for the many sins we've committed and commit in your blameless name) — she somehow remains a politically correct egalitarian.

Pretense is harder to sustain in Johnson Mills. In the great silence, amid the relentless rain of vacant moments, against the flawless sky of my loneliness, a lie stands out like a crow on a maple stripped of foliage. Here, each self-serving excuse, each sorry rationale announces itself, clashing with the harmonious chord of Maine's emptiness; here, you cannot help but begin to doubt yourself. (Are these the thoughts my father had as he made his rounds house to house?) Looking back now from my porch by the pond, from my station behind the register, I see more clearly the self-deceit which brought me here. I pretended that our department was clean; I pretended for awhile that I was earning our living; I pretended that I felt at home in Colton Falls, that my kisses and caresses retained some meaning.

In contrast to that self-sanitized past, this land has a sobering severity. Toadstools erupt like malignancies. Flies die in prodigious quantities, spilled on my sills like a cupful of raisins. The forest floor rots, a rank and damp, many-limbed corpse, fungus and moss feeding on the bark of failed aspirations. Soon, the pond's summer-soft surface will congeal, another harsh and reflective plane upon which I'll be forced to judge myself — I have no defense. Am I

25

pretending now that this letter, this confession, can make a difference?

When I left . . . no, when I *ran out* — like Mr. Bob, with his "minimum wage," I must learn to say the truth straight out — the Chief Inspector was the only one I told. I hadn't planned to tell him. I hadn't even planned my imminent desertion; didn't even know until I spoke what I was about to say or do. But after one more fight over finances, over another "loan" which Marjorie had accepted; after one more edgy truce, nothing said, another night spent our bodies going rigid when they accidentally touched in our queen-sized bed; after yet another rerun of my morning script, shaving by rote, dressing by rote, eating once again a muffin well-done with strawberry jam; after another anxious morning commute — my lifeline snapped. You knew, I believe, better than I. When I hugged you that morning, you began to cry. On the highway, I nearly ran a car off a bridge, fueled by a rage at an offense so small that my own instability frightened me, forcing me to pull off the road to collect myself as if I had drunk too much or were falling asleep.

At lunch the Inspector, proceeding according to inflexible custom, took no note of my disintegration. He ate, he talked, he made the usual complaint about his sausage sub's watery sauce, a subject which quickly led, following some thread of logic only he could comprehend, to yet another awe-struck saga of coercion and corruption in City Hall. Minutes passed as if torn from my flesh. I clutched a sandwich to my face, less out of any desire to eat than as a self-defense, a means to hide the desperate jerking of my claustrophobic eyes, their search for escape. I couldn't bear it, not just the story, not just the Inspector's predictable mythologizing, but the entire script: the door closed, the phone on hold, the awful sandwiches and debris-strewn desk. The very clutter seemed a threat. I had an irrational urge to straighten up, to throw away wrappers, to file folders, to line up corners, to brush back the Inspector's cowlick, plastering it flat against his head; I had a sudden craving for visual order, a need to make that room, that moment succinct, well-reasoned, and easily read.

But the clutter only grew worse, measured by a rising pile of crumpled napkins damp with sauce; the story cluttered, too, with irrelevant asides and meditations, unexpected reversals and repetitions, its plotline turned to macrame. And all so slow, so awed yet mild, all delivered in the Inspector's soft, pacific, porch-rocking style. Had I heard about the Mayor's file of vice squad pictures? *(Pause.)* Hadn't I known that a certain editor's son had been caught "with his pants down" in a public rest room? *(Pause, rock.)* In which case, then, how did I think the Mayor had won that paper's endorsement in the last election? *(Pause, rock; pause, smile.)* Which recalled, of course, how "hizzoner" had once bugged the phone of a local columnist, a man whose sister, by the way . . .

Again my lifeline snapped. Raging, I threw my uneaten sandwich onto the desk; threw it so hard that it landed with a *splat,* so hard that the soft bread split, bits of tuna salad ejected in a spray, adding yet one more layer to the accumulating mess. There was a pause. I froze, appalled. The Inspector, too, had stopped mid-word, his jaw hanging loose, a piece of mayo-dipped celery clinging to his shirt, and together we stared down, amazed, to the puddled remains, as if at a meteor fallen from outer space. How was I to explain myself?

"I'm quitting," I finally said.

"What?"

"I'm quitting," I said again; in a way, I was as shocked as he. Only with repetition did the words become real. "This job, I mean — I'm not coming back."

"You're what?" the Chief Inspector said. At last he drew his disbelieving eyes away from the desk; his cowlick protruded, bouncing, like a hitchhiker's thumb from the back of his head — if I just could have taken a brush to it.

"I'm going away — right now; today. I'm not coming back."

"Oh," he said. Only now had my meaning begun to sink in; disappointment and surprise held him, though, in a paralyzing equilibrium. The sauce from his sub, more brown than red, stained his hands. He had tucked a napkin under his chin, an improvised bib, which, when added to his boyish beardless face and his ever-present gentleness, gave him an aura of violated innocence, the wounded gaze of a friend betrayed. I was, after all, deserting him.

"It's my marriage," I rushed to explain. "It's Marjorie and her father, the sick little dance they perform together. Money, money, money; it's always money, money, money they're dancing to, making each other miserable. It's his life's project now, Daddy's last job, to prove that she's corruptible — and she is. *She is!* You wouldn't believe what she used to call her father — for Christsake, *I* was the one who had to calm her. Even now she'll rage against him hour after hour. But she submits; 'for Robbie's sake,' we always end up accepting the 'gift.' A gift with so many strings attached, so many silent caveats, so many new opportunities for the man to assert his influence . . ."

28

I paused, trying to catch my breath. I had merely meant to explain to the Inspector that there were personal reasons for my leaving and that I held him blameless, but the words had rushed out with a will of their own, out of control like the way I drove. And he sat there, stunned, his napkin still tucked under his chin, a hit-and-run victim of my careening confession blinking in embarrassment and disbelief.

"It's my marriage," I said again. I couldn't help myself, passive dummy to my own hysterical ventriloquist. A hand, hot from the friction, rubbed at my forehead furiously. "It's Colton Falls. It's the way my mother behaves when she enters our house. On her knees, she might as well be on her knees so awed is she by the things we own, by the fact that I live in Colton Falls. It makes me sick, that I've redeemed somehow her vision of success. It makes me sick, all those lawns so geometric, all those gizmos, grandiose utensils that fill our kitchen. Crock pots, yoghurt makers, lettuce driers, olive pitters — shit, all of it. *Shit!* I caught my mother gazing at our Cuisinart as if it were a museum piece. God spare me please, God please spare me one more possession, one more utterly useless shopping mall special . . ."

I slumped, my hand fell. "Money, money, money," I murmured to myself, winding down, but then I remembered last night's fight and the latest "loan." "Money, money, *money!*" I erupted again, and when I ended the refrain by slapping the desk, the Inspector flinched. "We don't talk these days — we count. We don't make love anymore — we're too busy taking inventory."

There was an abrupt pause. The frankness of that last revelation had startled even me and I shut up. Across the

29

desk the Inspector, blushing, cleared his throat: *his* eyes were now the claustrophobic ones, searching the room for a quick escape.

"You're upset," he said at last; he stared down, though, as if reading one of the memos which littered his desk.

"You don't have to . . . I mean, it isn't necessary for you to — "

"You're just upset, that's all it is."

"Yes, upset. But you shouldn't think . . . ."

I stopped, unwilling, unable to complete the thought. I had already said too much and was becoming aware that beyond embarrassing the Inspector with my pathetic confession, I had actually managed to offend him as well. There was a kind of pout about his features, a sullenness like a subtle bruise which lurked beneath his sympathy. And the source of this distress, I realized with amazement then, was less what I had said than when, the timing of my outburst and not its content. I was quitting without a moment's notice and he was upset because our tacit lunchtime rules had been broken, because I had interrupted his storytelling. The lunch hour was his, you see; *his* theater, *his* one-man play, the only portion of the working day over which he asserted his sovereignty, and I had dared to trespass on that territory. I had violated his myth-beclouded sanctuary with my hysterical complaint.

Ashamed, I turned away. The Inspector's reluctant show of sympathy, his almost grudging attempts to comfort me, seemed unbearably humiliating. I felt as if I had made a pass, at a woman far beneath my usual standards, who had nevertheless responded, indifferent to the honor I was bestowing upon her, with unremitting mockery: verbal scorn, theatrical boredom, uproarious laughter at my insufficient organ. That it should come to this, that I should have only the Chief Inspector to whom to confess, that I should prove so friendless, so desperate . . .

I stared to the floor. It had occurred to me with a stinging, self-stigmatizing certainty that this incident was no accident, that I *was* without friends, without confidants, that there *was* no one to tell my story to, not an adult left alive in the world whose comfort mattered, who had won my love without reservation. Whom was I trying to fool with this life of facile acquaintanceships, so many voices to hide the emptiness, the bogus charm and surface smiles of suburban neighbors and tennis partners, the Chief Inspector's storytelling? I was alone. Whether in Colton Falls or city hall, surrounded by hundreds or by myself, I was alone. And I felt alone then. It had struck like a drug, with an intravenous chilling rush, that recognition of my loneliness. My neck went rigid. I sensed my skin, as if a plastic shroud sealing me in, constrict and stiffen. With a new and almost disorienting clarity, I observed the room, its desk and chairs, its filing cabinets and coffee-maker, each object seeming, as it grew more vivid, to pull away, to withdraw from me like Marjorie's leg beneath the covers.

And all along, a voice wove itself in and out of my consciousness, an emerging score for the scene before me, a lyric for my loneliness. I knew it by heart, not just the tune, the words, but the very fingerprint of sound, the shape of the mouth which was its source. I knew it by heart, and yet recognition arrived like an unseen punch, forcing all the air from my lungs, bringing unexpected tears to my eyes, a sudden fear haunting the mind that I might have lost my sanity. Was it from without or within, an hallucination or a memory relived, this ghostly appeal over-

31

riding the years and the laws of possibility? So old and yet so powerful, so long forgotten and yet so immediate: my father's voice, unaccountably there, adorning the moment with a melody. My father singing.

At first I was sure that I had actually heard it, that rhythmic, rasping rise and fall of his unself-conscious baritone; at first I believed that I could actually feel the breath of his presence fill the room, just as it had so many years ago when I lay half-asleep in my childhood house, wondering what it meant to be a man. And for a moment, hope arrayed against reason, caught as if in that credulous state between dream and waking, I even searched the office for him. But it quickly passed. The sheer weight of reality relentlessly separated wishes from facts, forcing me to realize then that what I had heard was not the voice but its disappearance; that what I had felt, as with the body's vivid recollection of an amputated limb, was not my father but the absence of him, a resurrecting grief. And even then I continued to hear it, to feel it, that absence of music; in every pause, heard the unvoiced cry of what it was that was missing from my life, felt the loss of what had once been. My father was not singing — nor would he ever be again.

"You're upset," the Chief Inspector said, boy playing man, reluctant comforter of his subordinate-friend; squirming, he made an attempt at a reassuring smile. Although he knew his weaknesses better than I, his appointment by the Mayor protected him at least from the public perception of failure which had dogged my father most of his life.

"Yes," I said.

"You're just upset, that's all it is."

"Yes — upset."

My words were slow, soft. I didn't want to obscure even

that shadowy reminder of my father's voice. *You'll turn out just like him,* my mother would say in times of despair; *he'll turn out just like him,* she was fond of predicting during those long conversations with her conspiring sister: *two peas from a pod.* ("Underachiever" was the grandiloquent word that high school teachers would write on my card.) And yet we never looked alike — not like the Chapman kids and Mr. Bob. I used to stare at you, Rob, I used to stare and stare, trying to find myself in the color of your eyes, the curl of your hair. I used to search your face, hoping to retrieve, as if a reprieve, that misplaced cent, that mysterious, un-named chance that I'd lost. (Do we live again in our children? Can we be reborn?)

"If you'd just let yourself relax," the Chief Inspector said; (my father was thought a failure because he didn't possess a title like that), "if you could just step back and get away from things, take a day off and have a few drinks . . . Why, I remember a fight that Marie and I had — "

"I'm sorry," I broke in.

"Don't worry about it — I understand. Take some time off and you'll come back a new man. . . . *Women,*" he added, in a confiding manner, shaking his head.

"I'm sorry, I'm really very sorry, but I'm not coming back."

There was a pause. The Chief Inspector slumped, rocked back, that "man-to-man" expression sliding off his face.

"You're sure you — "

"I'm sure."

"We couldn't just leave it that you're on vacation, that there's an illness, say, an illness in — "

"I'm *sure,*" I said. And I was. I could already feel myself being drawn, that vacuum, that absence of music pulling me north. Out of city hall, out of Colton Falls, to this land of pine hills, paper mills, and impoverished soil — to the source of the song. The Inspector, though, still refusing to believe it, stared down to his phone with a look of dazed hope as if pondering a call to the cavalry.

"Listen to me," I said. "I know it isn't fair. I know that you deserve better than this, but you have to understand that I mean what I say. I really am leaving and you have to make plans: reorganize, find someone to take my place. . . . Bernstein would be best — don't you think? . . . Yes, Bernstein's the one who could handle it. I'll give him a call before I go. I promise you that I'll fill him in before I leave today, if you want me to. . . . Okay?"

I paused, staring at my boss, waiting in vain for the slightest sign of a positive response. Nothing about him had changed. Not the improvised bib, not the sauce-stained hands, not that vacant stare, both stunned and hurt, which blurred his face — like some silly 3-D logo, the piece of celery from my sandwich still clung to his shirt. Where would he have been, what would this poor man ever have done, if he hadn't had the Mayor's cousin for a wife?

"Please — for your own sake. You have to understand that I mean what I say, that I'm not coming back."

But in his own fashion, he did understand. It turned out that in my panic and my guilt I had overestimated my importance to the man, that I had failed to see the genius behind his passivity — its capacity to absorb, like the ocean a storm, any and all agencies of change. I would leave, but he would remain the same. Although it was true that my desertion had hurt him, he had, as a defeatist, come to expect such disappointments and in a certain sense enjoyed them: they confirmed for him his despairing views; they provided him an enduring rationale for his generalized surrender to the world. Unwilling to resist, he was by nature quick to accept, quick to forget. By the time I had made my call to Bernstein, he already appeared to have resigned himself to the fact that I was leaving him. The stunned stare faded. He returned to his sandwich. That ruminative smile which I had learned to expect in days gone by even made an appearance. For him, if not for me, the momentum of a thousand past lunches was taking over; slowly, incredibly, as if nothing at all had just taken place, the whole tedious ritual was re-emerging: just another normal day with the door closed, the phone on hold, the Inspector's words coiling themselves like a sun-doped snake around his audience of one — an audience which waited, condescendingly patient, for his asphyxiating hour-long monologue to end.

Did I remember the time we had found hidden in our files a stack of citations over thirty years old? (*Pause.*) Or how about the time we'd inspected that Portuguese restaurant and found all the basement wiring exposed? (*Pause, rock.*) I hadn't known, had I, that the real motivation behind that spot inspection was that the Mayor's mistress had once lived with the restaurant's owner? (*Pause, rock; pause, smile.*) Which reminded him of the time we'd both attended, upon threat of suspension, a charity ball sponsored by the Mayor's wife, only to find . . .

Increasingly amazed, caught in some spiritual limbo between Trenton and Maine, I listened. Already, as if we were old army buddies or fraternity brothers, he was talking about "the times" we had had together; already for him I had ceased to exist, absorbed by him out of the risky realm of the present tense and into the magical sphere of his reminiscence where all things were rendered wonderous but safe. Before my own eyes, I was being transformed into myth; reduced to fodder for his ongoing saga, an especially touching chapter about a young idealist who'd been hounded by Hizzoner from public service. The Inspector warmed to his words. Watching him rock, watching him pause, watching that ruminative smile dawn and die, poses I'd seen so many times before, I was forced to admit that he'd survived intact, survived not just my resignation but my entire four-year term as his right-hand man. For all my condescension, *he* had trained *me* and not vice versa; for all its weaknesses, *his* had actually proven to be the stronger personality. I hadn't changed him in the least. He was the same now and would remain the same after I left; would within the week, I realized then, stunned by my own irrelevance, have Bernstein trained to take my place. For all the difference it made, I might have been Bernstein myself, sitting there then, indulging the Inspector, listening to endless tales about my predecessor; just another mute audience of one attempting to suppress an urge to yawn, while the door remained closed, the phone on hold, the sauce-stained napkins piling up.

At last, at long last, the lunch came to an end. The transition from fantasy to fact, from lunch to life, was never very pleasant for the Chief Inspector, but he seemed to find the prospective exchange of our final goodbyes an especially daunting circumstance. A great reluctance overcame him. Like the child he in some ways was, wanting to pretend that nothing in life must come to an end, he began to stall, nervously repeating the most obvious lies: that we'd keep in touch; that he and Marie would have me over to their house; that if I stayed in town, we could still manage somehow to meet for lunch. But as alone as I had ever been, never more aware that things, that people, do come to an end, I couldn't assist him in sustaining that pretense and he quickly sank into silence again.

Finally I stood up; offered him my hand. Rising reluctantly, he accepted it and we stood there together, both silent, both sad, our hands clasped over his desk, aware that we would not meet again. Outside, a phone began to ring and I turned to leave. The Inspector, with a touching urgency, strengthened his grip, holding me in place. Ours had been a friendship of convenience, a friendship based on mutual weakness, but a friendship nonetheless; and a kindly, sentimental man, he didn't want to let it pass without some sort of eulogy. Words for once, though, would not come. Embarrassed, he avoided my eyes, frowning, smiling, frowning again, scanning the room nervously as if searching for a script to read, our uneasy pause stretching on and on until, a solution found, he reached down slowly to the surface of his desk.

For a moment I misunderstood. For a moment I thought that he was retreating again, into a reassuring forgetfulness, pretending somehow that nothing had changed, our agenda the same, business-as-usual according to the rules of our tacit arrangement: for just a moment I was sure that he was about to transfer another stack of memos to his right-hand man. But I was wrong. I had, as I had for four years running, failed to appreciate the complexity of my boss. For what he retrieved for me then from the wreckage of his desk was not a stack of memos but an unexpectedly perceptive good-bye gift — half joke, half parting advice, the truest memento of our city hall life.

What he handed me then, as if the baton in a relay race we could not win, was that oddly appropriate PLAN AHEad sign . . . and yet the fog was slow to burn off in my mind.

Memo to Myself. Subject: A Letter to My Son, Robert Douglas, Age One Year, Nine Months. A.2. Explain Self— apologize . . . Dear Son, dear Robbie, my Son: I'm sorry, so sorry that I didn't plan ahead, sorry that my life in its sloppiness has come to resemble the Inspector's desk; for it occurs to me now, too late, as my mind begins to clear while I wait at my station two towns south of Little Chester, that you alone are the chance that I've lost. Are you all right? Is there something you need, a present, an answer, some fatherly advice? I know that this won't work. I know that an apology is the true "minimum wage," the least you deserve. And what I fear, Rob, is that you won't survive the winter on such niggardly pay; that you, too, will find someone else, a stand-in, a Bernstein, to take my place. But . . . but if . . . but if you could just . . .

2.

"Robin's Nest," two miles south of Rte. 45. A lakefront cottage "nestled among the pines." Sleeps six. Fireplace, shower, screened porch and all utensils. Electric heat. Dock, canoe, child-safe beach. Clean air, privacy, trails nearby. *Must be seen!* Write Box 28 or call 589-6365.

And so easy to find. After a suitable pause for your check to clear, directions will arrive: detailed, typewritten, filled with folksy parenthetical enthusiasms, unexpected asides. Take the Turnpike north to the Canby exchange ("Try the spring water there!"). Go west on 23, past the Forestry Office and the creamery ("Watch out for the deer!"), on through the intersection at Kimberly another twenty-six miles. Follow 8A into Afton, through Budapest, Rockwell, Crosby Station ("Keep on pluggin', you've almost made it!"), bearing north and west on Rte. 45, about seventeen miles, till you enter the village of Johnson Mills, where you're then advised to ("Stop in at the Trader, stock up on provisions, and ask Bob Chapman how they're bitin'!"). — The perch, that is, not the black flies.

From the village you're instructed, as if some sort of

religious pilgrim, to "follow the signs." These, it turns out, will lead you south, to a short dirt road veined with roots, across a peninsular bulge in the scythe-shaped pond. There, at the water's edge, where the narrow road comes to an end, you'll pause to take in the enormous sky. It's over, you've arrived. And your long flight north seems to have brought you at last that refuge you sought "nestled among the pines": the canoe, the porch, the private beach, they're all there as advertised. Dazed, the hum of the car's engine still haunting your ears, you start inside. The key, you read, glancing to the bottom of your instruction sheet, has been "hidden" on the frame above the door, an absurdity which inspires a smile. Security, you perceive, like the hellos you receive, is perfunctory here, a nod to form. Only later, if you linger past the summer vacation, does the meaning of security begin to become clearer: it is not man that is most feared in the province of the Yankee Trader.

"Robin's Nest," two miles south of Rte. 45. A crow's proprietary caw, outraged at some trespass, rattles the dawn, jarring me awake. A seam of light splits the curtains, a milky intrusion; and my eyes blinking open, I absorb through the window a vertical strip of shore and sky. A sun-struck cloud, a wedge of lily-spotted pond, a nuthatch pecking its breakfast upside down on a scabrous pine; tufts of weed, dead needles, water-darkened sand — they impress themselves before I know who I am. The room remains dark. A hundred other bodies having broken it in like so many fists punching a pocket in a baseball mitt, my bed is sunken and soft. Stirring, I yawn. For a long lazy moment, I'm still unable to place myself. But then, when I stretch and the bed's spartan blanket begins to scratch my unprotected chest, *hair shirt,* an antiquated term abruptly understood, explodes like the cry of the crow into consciousness: I know who I am. And so it is that each man, each age, must learn the penance of grief all over again.

The morning has broken cold; my cold feet, protesting, dance arthritically across the floor. My father was the one whose job it was to wake me up for school — my name softly spoken, followed by a knock on my bedroom door. "Another day," he would sometimes say, an observation he made without the slightest sign of either hope or despair. (What was the source, how did he evolve such an all-abiding serenity?) In the mirror now above the sink, hearing the accelerating thump of the water pump's beat, I see him shaving; admire again that flair he brought to his morning preparations, the razor poised like a scalpel in his hand, that uniform which made his "failure" indiscreet — the blue shirt, the cap, the gray striped pants with a cluster of keys hanging from the hip — folded neatly across a chair. *He works for the government,* my mother would explain, intentionally vague, hoping to evoke unnamed positions of power and prestige: ambassadorships, confidential advisers to presidents. But such deliberate ambiguity was hard to sustain with a husband who walked out the door each day wearing the blue and gray of the postal service.

House to house on those weekday mornings, he would walk his route. Stroke by stroke, cutting effortless swaths in the lather on his face, he would shave himself — he made it seem so enviable. Tapping my razor against the sink, I remember the way he would present each cheek to the bathroom mirror, examining them slowly for subtle errors — nicks, missed whiskers, spots of lather; there was no flaw too small to escape the scrutiny of his craftsman's standards. So intense was his testing gaze that when, at

41

last, he splashed his face with aftershave, it seemed a kind of christening, an official, almost religious sanctioning of the job completed. Awed, I would watch him from the doorway. There were mornings even when, impatient with my beardlessness, I would sneak in after him to reenact the ceremony: the creamy lather; the smooth strokes with a bladeless razor; that final solemn consecration. And the thrill I felt then, with the first cleansing chill of the aftershave (it was light blue, I recall, its strong scent a dizzying mix of spiced citrus and alcohol), arose less from playing at the rituals of manhood than from a borrowed sense of my father's approval, as if I, too, through that magical touch of lotion to skin, had managed to pass those standards of craft which mattered more than "success" to him.

The water drains, the memories fade. Outside, the raucous crow erupts again — the pond is his alone, he seems to say. The absence of approval, like the absence of music, is everywhere, and yet requires a still eye, a quiet soul to be appreciated. Exile, I've learned, is for the discriminating: the dry wine of pain.

Well-trained, I rinse off the razor, the sink, return the aftershave to the cabinet. The water pump slows, then stops while I'm drying my hands and, like an indrawn breath upon a precipice, the great Maine silence invades again. My ears adjust; I freeze above the sink; something stirs, faintly heard, on the northern fringes of consciousness. For just a moment I feel called, hoping for a new "event" to calibrate my life — but I've been fooled. The sound, I quickly learn, is the familiar sound of the status quo. It's always here, the very voice of the town, the stain of mankind upon the wilderness. It's always here for the discriminating ear, like the sense of guilt I've come to feel: that perpetual perpetual hum of the mill.

More flies have died on the sills. (Were they trying to escape or, sensing death, did they choose a romantic final resting place — a grave with a view?) One step from the bathroom, "Robin's Nest" presents itself. With its open space; with its utilitarian furnishings and stone fireplace; with its subtle cabin scent of wet wood and cold ash; with that slightly seedy atmosphere geared to a certain species of vacationer, delighted to be "roughing it." The ceiling is low. The floor, covered with nondescript linoleum, is on a tilt. The walls, lined with horizontal planks of pine, are not quite squared; oddly, they are only two-thirds stained, the task abruptly terminated mid-wall, mid-stroke, as if the owner had run out of money, will, or vacation days.

My father would have shaken his head at such lackadaisical workmanship. My mother, drawing industry from shame, would enact an energetic campaign of camouflage: hand-sewn curtains, home-grown plants, expensive wallpaper found on sale — humiliation has made her a "handy" woman. Under her direction, the modest house we shared was in a constant state of reclamation. There was something almost heroic about the way she persisted in trying to rescue an aura of status from my father's indifference and limited income. *You are what you own* was and is her core belief and the ruling ethic of Colton Falls; *you are who you control* was the version valued at city hall. Here I control no one, own next to nothing; even the things I rent add up to a scanty, secondhand inventory — the stuff of yard sales in this impoverished country. There's a drop-leaf table. There's a propane stove. There's a single toaster, as squat and bulbous as a thirties' roadster, its cord sheathed in cloth like a modest matron's opaque hosiery. There are seven forks, six spoons, a few dull steak knives with handles made of imitation bone, a spatula, a hand eggbeater (no *Cuisinarts,* no olive pitters); the enamel, sponge-dulled, has yellowed on the refrigerator. The living room, too, is lacking in glamour. On its walls, bits of angler esoterica: a net, a "Gone Fishin'" plaque, a chart depicting species native to the continent. On its floor, dilapidated furniture: a few mismatched chairs, a frayed braided rug, a lamp, a footstool, a sagging sofa whose soft upholstery seems to exude a dampness born of too many pond-soaked bathing suits. By the door, alone, there's a plain black phone which never rings.

To this, I've added little of my own. Some clothes, a book or two, the music box my father made — the letter he wrote. On the mantel above the fireplace, beside a black-and-white photo of the owner and his wife, I've placed the Inspector's PLAN AHEad sign. Renting is so strange; I feel, on alternating days, either at home or an invader here, the caretaker of other people's lives.

It's a Tuesday, about seven a.m. Sunlight, silvery still, filters through the pines, the curtains and slowly brightens the dark recesses of Robin's Nest. It's a Tuesday, my assigned day of rest: today alone, no register, no squeaking planks, no millhands to cash their meager checks; today alone and yet I bend already beneath the burden of my idleness. I've shaven, I've dressed. Not hungry, I hold a cup of coffee in my hand. Aimless, I walk from the living room to the kitchen and back again. Days off are the worst: I sit and rock, sit and rock, watch the summer die from my screened-in porch, watch the relentless subtraction of birds, leaves, busyness, and warmth. I sit and rock.

44

The sun has yet to clear the hills. A few late water lily blossoms, pink cups on saucers, remain clenched like buds against the chill. Across the inlet, shallow currents, ruffling the water's glycerine surface, betray a wind I cannot feel. Days off are the worst: there's too much empty time to fill.

I wonder, rocking, what to do — take a walk? drive to town? read a book? as a penance, chant my many failings to myself? Superstitiously, I resist taking out the canoe. It's almost as if I fear the loss of solid ground, as if without it, without Dad or Rob — without the physical proximity, the gravity of love — I would drift away, cease utterly to be, dissolve like a morning fog in this land of lakes. On Tuesdays, I begin to feel unreal.

Back home in Colton Falls, and in the Connecticut town where I grew up, days off were prized. "Free time" was the dessert, the drug-of-choice, one's chance to "enrich" an ordinary life. Recreation assumed the air of religion; to enjoy oneself was a moral obligation. There arose, both at work and home, a kind of idolatry of the Weekend — to do nothing, to have no plans, was an embarrassment, a lapse verging on sacrilege. Tennis dates, dinner parties, trips to ski slopes, stays at inns with other couples; to have fun, to keep busy, to buy something, to face the bleak descent of Sunday evening by preparing already for the following weekend — phone calls made, names penned into open squares on the calendar. Leisure required industry; it demanded, as a college coach of his football players, an unrepentant enthusiasm.

Here, too, people keep busy, although they hide (from me at least) the gimcrack joy of the hobbyist, although the ideal they pursue, as a consequence of their solitude, is not "enrichment" but a form of self-sufficiency. There's wood to

45

split, there are cars to fix, men elbow-deep in the oily innards of their pickup trucks; there are gardens to tend. The hunting season — birds, then deer — will soon begin. For entertainment, they visit neighbors or drive thirty miles to the nearest drive-in movie theater or take in the races at Rockwell Speedway. Like everyone else, they indulge themselves with sex and drinking — (see Bob Chapman, State Liquor Agent). There are prayer meetings, there's a 4-H chapter; fairs are held throughout the summer. Every week, at one church or another, there seems to be a potluck supper.

I do not attend — races, fairs, church events. I own no gun, have no garden, will have to rely on Mr. Bob if my car malfunctions. I am, it becomes increasingly clear, less a neophyte native than a stranded stranger: a man out of sync and out of season, between two places and at home in neither.

The owner, in his own touchingly inept way, has tried to anticipate my predicament, taping to the wall beside the refrigerator a "Things To Do" list for the restless, the bored, the unimaginative renter. Predictably, half the suggestions are related to fishing and, like his directions, each one ends — emblazoned more than punctuated, struck as if with a slap on the back from a hearty uncle — with the slash and dot of an exclamation. "Take a ramble in the woods out to Guymann's Point!" "Paddle out past the bridge and try casting to the southern side of the man-shaped rock!" In the bedroom closet, as a hedge against rainy-day boredom, he's stored some games: a cribbage board, playing cards, Parcheesi, checkers, Clue, something called War of the Worlds. There's a children's book, a Nancy Drew, within which some vacationing girl, showing a tenacity

46

beyond her years, has crossed out with crayon the heroine's name wherever it appears, scrawling in its place her own — Helene. There are times when I feel so close. There are times when every object here seems a revelation in itself, the puzzle piece of some larger truth.

My coffee cools. More leaves fall. A chipmunk, busy with his own list of "Things To Do," forages frantically outside the porch. Two months are enough to be forewarned; the waiting will only get worse, I know, time turning almost palpable — heavy, edgy, unfulfilled, like the air before a thunderstorm.

Rising from my chair, with the vague intention of "taking a ramble" either around the pond or, as the owner suggested, through the woods to Guymann's Point, I step outside. There, I pause. Helplessly, my plans delayed, I'm drawn away from the shaded path toward the sun-glazed pond: its lilies, its glassy morning stillness, its stalks, its weeds, its half-submerged, gray-bleached trees have come to embody my sense of loss. Slowly, sadly, I approach the dock. I know, hating what I know as I cross the sand, that I'll have to stop, that I've come as far as I can — to Johnson Mills, Maine; to the water's edge. Staring down from the end of the dock, I examine my face as, for so many mornings, my father did his. It was here, on this beach, by this dock, gazing across this very pond, here little more than a month before, that I came closest to reviving him. It was here, "nestled among the pines," that for just one moment everything I'd done seemed justified — even leaving Rob behind.

It was July, late July. Rain had fallen hard the night before, toadstools shredded like wind-ripped umbrellas, the beach sand cut with canals of erosion, but the morning had risen clear and bright. I had been for a swim, out to a distant rock and back again, following the channels and avoiding the weeds, through shallow water riddled with the dark darting shadows of bluegills and minnows, their sun-struck scales flashing like tin. Exhausted from the lap, I waded back in. Using my towel as a pillow, I dropped, stomach-down, onto the beach where, limp and damp, I surrendered myself to the sun and the sand, to the midsummer heat. Sleep, my only ambition then was to rest, to sleep. I had been lulled during those first bright days of my stay in Maine by a brief, beguiling sense of peace. It was still July; the relief of my escape was still fresh in my mind; my separation from Robbie, although painful and frightening, still seemed to me then less a sentence than a trial — a trial I might win. I had a faith in those beginning days, or if not exactly faith, then an unexamined hope that "things" would work out, that I just might succeed.

Robin's Nest, two miles south of Rte. 45. On the cusp of midday, at the end of July. Belly down, on the beach, my stillness measured in degrees of heat, my limbs beginning to liquefy.

Minuscule waves brushed against the shore. Dragon-flies hovered and zipped, slashes of blue iridescence with cellophane wings; they mated, double-decker, their abdomens pinched, on the dark green pads, on the glittering sand, moving as one through the dry bright air. Sparrows chirruped in the trees. A robin, increasingly inured to my motionless form, hopped and pecked about the fringes of the beach. Beside me and behind me, throughout the plant-dense expanse of the sheltered inlet, I could hear the fish feed; heard the splash and ripple as they pierced the surface to swallow a meal, the stillness broken, too, by the graceless

48

plops of bellyflopping frogs, the squawk of a duck, the liquid gurgle of a tail fin's wash as it chased or escaped in the shallow water along the shore. And more, always more. Loud or soft, near or far, always a new event with its own specific tone and pitch, its own localizing coordinates in the tapestry of sound which described the pond — while the sun beat down and the sparrows called and a series of waves from some unseen boat or a breeze not felt gently *slapped-slapped-slapped* against the dock.

I closed my eyes. In a strange way then I seemed to divide, caught on the seesawing scales of body and mind : my torso sinking, ever more limp, ever more liquid; my mind floating high — still, lucid, serenely receptive. There were no thoughts, no associations. Judgments had been replaced by pure perception; the self had become a star-lit sky of precise sensations, that tapestry of sound growing clearer and clearer. With every stir in the pond, a life was being taken, with each subtle splash a water bug gone, a fingerling eaten; life and death, life and death, dragonflies mating acrobatically above my head, hatchlings hidden away in their arboreal nests. Everything fit. Everything was what it was necessarily, neither more nor less. Even the hum of the mill seemed part of the score, an integral, essential harmonizing voice. And all along as the sounds became clearer — the trills of the birds, the incessant feeding — my sun-struck body felt more and more liquid, in the process of sinking, as if, like last night's rain, I were being drawn down through the sand and filtered clean; brought back, in some ceaseless cycle of replenishment, to the life-soup of the pond from whence I came.

The sun beat down. I felt myself dissolve, my mind, though, ever more attuned to the pulse of the pond, ever

49

more aware that something special was happening, an almost mystical process, the last leg of my long journey. Close, I was drawing so close. On the verge, it seemed, of bypassing its shield of taciturn people and being absorbed directly by the land itself. If I could just remain as I was, a passive captive of sand and sun, if I could just continue to blend in with the hot pond shore — insects crawling across my arms, the robin inured to my motionless form — I might pass through to the other side: native, not stranger; brought to the source of my father's singing. I scarcely breathed, afraid to move. Every sound seemed a sign, a note which deepened the expectant mood. Blinking open my eyes, gazing across the sand, I caught for a moment a vision of life on a smaller scale: the relentless hunting of spiders and ants, a caravan bearing a beetle's corpse, life and death, life and death, while a wren *kip-kipped* its warning from the brush and the trees above, as if heeding its call, ceased to sway, not a hint of a breeze to stir the air.

A daddy longlegs strode across the sand. Abruptly, wrenching my limbs out of their lethargy, I pushed myself up and whirled toward the pond. Something had happened — *would* happen; with a flash of intuition, cued by some subliminal shift in the tapestry's pattern, I knew to turn at just that moment.

One arm propped me up. A thin armor of damp sand clung to my chest and my bathing trunks. Squinting, I stared out, waiting for some unknown climax to enact itself, trying to parse from the scrambled syntax of shore and sky a bit of coherence, a frame to shape the inscrutable face of the wilderness. There was a brief but unbearable delay. My searching eyes began to ache, my free hand rising, an improvised visor, against the dazzling aqueous midday glare. Then, without warning, it arrived; then, with all the miraculousness of consciousness, an image born, torn out of nothingness, I was given my sign. Something large and vivid, cutting across my field of vision. Something huge, slate blue, wings driving the air with smooth, slow, powerful strokes — something unaccountable in its beauty. A heron in flight.

I held my breath. As if aware of its passage, the entire inlet seemed to pause, soundless, breezeless, in a gesture of awe, as the heron shot straight across the heart of the pond, just a few feet above the water's surface. Its beak speared the air, pointing the way. Its long neck was flexed, its eyes were fixed, its skull was little more than a socket for them — a slender bulb designed to slip through the strongest winds. The slow beat of its enormous wings, the manifest ease with which they maintained its buoyancy, seemed to express an unself-conscious sovereignty. The primal rule of a creature perfectly adapted to its given world. The dominion of grace on a planet of stone.

I didn't move. Only my eyes traced its line of flight to the opposite shore where the slate-colored bird began to slow — its body tilting, its stilt-legs dropping, its wings turned to brakes, cushioning its descent to a fallen tree which, long ago stripped of bark and leaves, lay half-submerged like a reclining nude in the shallow water. There, the long neck unfolded. There, the wings, drawing in, pressed against its slender body. There, its roost secured, the wild bird froze, a slight ruffling of its tail, a minute adjustment in the angle of its head the last discernible lifelike motions. It was there. It was gone. It was there, then gone: even as I stared, the incredible had happened, the event dissolving before my eyes. It was there; it was gone. Within a moment of its landing, the heron had so sunk into its marshy setting (gray feathers blending with gray weathered wood, its attenuated body a natural extension of the dead tree trunk) that it seemed to have vanished — transformed, as if by a magician's flourish, into just one more lifeless, leafless, bark-stripped branch.

I blinked in disbelief. More than an uncanny act of camouflage, the bird — so huge, so compelling only seconds before — actually seemed to have disappeared. It required an act of concentration bordering on faith, depending as much on memory as on sense, to extract a heron then from the visual array of weeds, trunk, water, and sand, to find the living bird in the still tableau of the midsummer day. And yet I continued to stare, eyes squinting, blinking against the glare. To me, dumb witness on the beach, that abrupt transition from bird to branch, from life to death, from perfect motion to perfect stillness, that seamless shift from pageantry to anonymity, seemed more awesome yet than the flight itself, more subtly profound; it seemed, I couldn't help but feel, to embody or suggest the very truth I had come to find. Haunted, I replayed and replayed the transformation in my mind. It was there. It was gone. It was there, then gone. It merged, this majestic bird, it submerged within its world — *it belonged.*

And for one brief moment then as I stared across the pond, I felt my father's presence so strongly that it seemed as if *he* were the one who had caught my eye, as if *his* were the soul which had winged its way from motion into stillness, from life into death, completing the passage with such quiet mastery, such elemental grace. And for that moment, brought so close to the spirit of the man, to the heart of the land, I could almost accept it. I could almost sense the inherent, the natural beauty of his death; see how it fit, see how it was what it was necessarily, neither more nor less. I could almost absorb even his loss as just one more thread in the tapestry of sound, another harmonizing note in the music of the whole, the music of the pond. Almost.

The tree remains. On the still water below the dock, beside a floating leaf, a seven-lobed oak, I examine my face: no, Dad and I, Rob and I, we don't look the same. What's passed on between a father and a son is so much more subtle and strong than the width of a smile or a family name, and it's just those invisible bonds, affinities of style, that I've come here to trace. After the event itself, the heron's brief flight, I began to regard my little harbor in the pond as a sacred place; every rock, every fallen branch, the most inanimate of things, because they were there, seemed charged with spirit and capable of change. Day after day, like the boy who sought the thrill of his father's approval by mimicking the ritual of his morning shave, I would return to the beach, hoping to regain through a superficial reenactment of what had taken place — the swim, the wading in, the passive surrender to the midday heat — the magic of a moment which had faded away: its stillness, its clarity, its sense of peace.

The tree remains. Even now, two months too late, I try to conjure from its branches the heron's shape. Even now, I try to resurrect the elegant attenuation of its elongated neck, the enfolding wings, the paradox of its change from perfect motion to perfect stillness, the way it could both celebrate and be the pure expression of a place, a moment. But the heron is gone. Gone along with the ducks, the migratory geese, the downy woodpeckers, the finches, evening grosbeaks, the foreign cars with their out-of-state plates. July has become September, the sun a paler, cooler version of itself. The water bugs have vanished. The fish, breaking the surface less and less, have been forced into a silent abstinence. Everywhere I turn there are cocoons and abandoned nests, emblems of desertion and readiness. Every morning when I rock, the empty shells of insects killed by the frost are blown like chaff against the mesh of my screened-in porch. So many voices have been lost. The pond is muted. In a month, there'll be snow. Once again the absence of music.

My face, floating beside the leaf, ripples with a breeze. Self-examination, I've learned, is a subtle thing. If I stare too hard or too long, I'll lose that fragile reflection of myself and see straight through to the bottom of the pond, immersed in a murky montage of mud and sand, pale weed strands, and shadowy fish.

There's so little time and so little makes sense. Even though the sun has cleared the hills, the northern breeze carries a chill, the few remaining water lily blossoms opening now to hoard the light. Watching them from the dock, I frown, then turn. Faintly, in the distance, I've begun to hear, as if a native drum sounding its alarm throughout the land, the *thud-thud-thud* of an axe cutting wood. Trying to track it, I close my eyes, cock my ear. Sound is so elusive here; depending on the wind, it can die at its source or travel miles and miles through the open air, following the course of the waterways. The truth is, I know, it could be coming from almost anywhere — that relentless beat, that rhythmic violent preparation. No, it's not man that is most feared in the province of the Yankee Trader.

Pivoting on the dock, I turn away from the pond. I know now that I won't "take a ramble," after all, that I'll return to the porch where I'll sit and rock, sit and watch: no car to fix, no garden to tend, the end of summer's initiative — no son to kiss. The cold has sunk in, numbing my steps, as slowly I approach the cabin I rent; make my hunched retreat to the higher ground of Robin's Nest. Fireplace. Shower. Screened porch and all utensils. My rustic sill, the ledge from which I watch the world. Did I come here to escape, or was I choosing a romantic final resting place — a grave with a view?

I step across the sand. Masked by a cloud, the day takes on a grayer shade, a more circumspect air. Ahead, the chipmunk scrounges in the brush; it digs, scatters leaves, begins to freeze, then scurries across the flank of a dead tree trunk, the air rasped by the urgent scratch of his tiny claws against the bark. For him: neither hope nor despair. For him: just "another day," to be lived as it's lived necessarily, according to the harsh arithmetic of self-sufficiency. It's occurred to me lately that a heron in Trenton would be an ugly thing, that its beauty arose from its given home, from the perfect fit of form to place: born to a planeless sky, born to skim across a Maine lily pond in late July.

My father was born two towns to the north. His life, in retrospect, seems to me now indecently short. He was here; he was gone. He was here, then gone — and before I could learn exactly what it was, behind the silent front, which made him so strong. I've begun to wonder these days, as the songbirds flee and the turned leaves fall, if my coming here was wrong, if it's possible to change; wonder if, like Helene, I've been trying to impose my name, crudely with crayon, in another's given place.

The chipmunk doesn't care. Not what I think, who I am, not why I am here. Nibbling nervously on a mushroom cap, he starts at my approaching steps and then scrambles away, his escape, however, drawing my attention to some larger tracks which cut across the fringe of the sand. Automatically I redirect my path. Like some indigenous script, a secret message pressed on the blank page of the beach, the line of feral prints stretches off to my left. Reaching their end, I kneel down on the sand and, huddling there against the cold, begin to examine the last shallow print with a trembling hand. I must. I can't hold back. Even now, hope heading south, I must keep on trying to understand; even now, long past July, I must persist in trying to "follow the signs."

I freeze — on the sand, on my knees — when a hawk-sized crow, wheeling above, rips the silence with an outraged cry. There are two translations to what he says: That the pond is his. That it is not mine.

3.

Dear Son: I'm sorry, but I still can't seem to pull this off. So many words have been written and I still remain lost. So many mistakes made, false starts taken, so many years spent answering memos in the Department of the Housing Inspector and yet I still haven't managed to organize my thoughts. Already my outline's been undone. I have, in my confusion, tackled A.2. before A.1. I've rushed ahead, penitent, trying to explain away the son before explaining the father who helped make him what he was — the father who is gone; the grandfather, Rob, you never saw; the man who wrote the letter now housed in the music box he made, on the mantel above the fireplace, beside the black-and-white photo of the owner and his wife and the Chief Inspector's PLAN AHEad sign. If only the fog would clear from my mind . . .

The letter is dated *October, 1943;* it begins "Dear Son" and *I'm* the son who is being addressed, although, like you now, Rob, I was far too young then to know how to read — barely a month old, my father scarcely a man himself, drafted out of college and shipped overseas. On a bureau in

57

the bedroom they shared, my mother still displays a photo taken of him during those early days: days when she still believed she had married the man who would realize her dreams; days when the uniform he wore, unlike the blue and gray of the postal service, evoked that pride in him she wanted to feel. The photograph was, for its time, a standard one. With his formal pose and uniform, with his neutral expression, his beardless complexion, his air of unstamped innocence, the young second lieutenant pictured there could have been almost any American husband or son old enough to fight the war. The letter, too, was standard for its day. With so many men overseas, new fathers to children they had never seen, it became something of a convention for soldiers to send home a letter to their newborn daughter or son, expressing their love, explaining their absence, the necessity of defending democracy against the Nazis, letters that could be read much later—say, on a child's twelfth birthday — just in case they didn't come back from the war they fought in Europe or Asia or Africa.

My father did come back, although by the time I first saw him I was nearly one-and-a-half. In the years that followed till the time of his death, my mother, a shameless romantic, would on any occasion which teased her memory — an old TV movie, a Lennon Sisters' song, the funerals of Churchill, Eisenhower, MacArthur, and DeGaulle — whip out that letter and embarrass my father and myself by reading it aloud. My father was not an eloquent man, not a man of words. Written before he had actually seen combat, the content of the letter, like the picture on the bureau, has an unstamped, standardized innocence to it, a predictable form. Nevertheless, no matter how many times she had read it before, my mother would, by the end of her performance, be blinking back tears and swallowing sobs—although one could never be sure whether it was the letter itself or the nostalgia it evoked, grief for a time when her vision of life still seemed possible, which saddened her so.

Dad, meanwhile, would refuse to move, a statue in his chair. Following his example, I, too, would sit there mutely, eyes averted, hands to my brow like a parishioner in church posing for prayer. And the dismay we felt then, the wordless suffering we shared during those periodic eruptions of melodrama, always seemed to me proof of our secret bond, a sign of that affinity of style which, stronger than the silence keeping us apart, made us father and son.

On the day I left you — *ran out* — as I drove through Connecticut on a path that would end in Johnson Mills, there were only two things I snuck from my mother's house: one of the music boxes my father made (a maple beauty cut to the shape of a treasure chest; an exquisite miniature perfect in every feature, with leather strap hinges, seamless corners, and an antique filigreed gold lock and key) and, unexpectedly, unsure at first what attracted me, that letter he had written from overseas.

Finding it was a surprise. Rushing through my mother's bedroom, trying to escape before she came home, I spotted it on the bureau, out of its envelope and half unfolded, lying at the foot of that wartime photo as if the text to a sacred shrine. And it occurred to me then, with a sudden flood of sympathy, that she must still be reading that letter aloud, still blinking back tears and swallowing sobs, only now she would be crying alone — a widow, with an out-of-state son, in an empty house, performing before an audience of ghosts.

In the quiet of the bedroom, as if a time-softened echo,

I could almost hear her cry. The endurance of her love, I began to comprehend, dwarfed even mine. Touched, my vision of her changed. The embarrassment I had always felt in relation to the letter, the shame occasioned by her tearful readings, quickly slipped away. For the first time then as I lifted those familiar pages in my hand, I began to sense what my mother always sensed, the power they possessed to revivify the past; saw the letter as she saw it, more talisman than object, a secret door in time's prison wall which could lead me back, beyond the brink of death, to that second lieutenant who had returned from the war a stranger to us both. It was from *him,* you see — from him to me. Fresh from the Inspector's office, suffering from my own renewed and implacable sense of mourning, I craved some tangible connection to the man himself, to the father who was gone. And even though its content had an un-stamped, standardized innocence to it, the letter still seemed — because it came from his hands, because it was written in his script and addressed to me — to possess the necessary resurrecting quality. Even though it didn't tell me what I wanted to know, no answers to the mysteries which were and are tormenting me so, it still seemed an authentic emblem of his legacy to me — the perfect memento for my own small shrine.

Only later did the legacy become clear. It wasn't until later, on the verge of September, when the illusory peace had passed, giving way to guilt, and the magic of the heron seemed more and more remote, that I was ready to receive the inspiration. It was a Tuesday, my day of rest. Rain fell steadily, slapping the leaves, as I paced the cabin fitfully, the water drunk up by the porous sand. More than ever I was estranged from the land. There would be, I knew, if the bad weather held, no chance to take a ramble, no new attempt at a reenactment, confined all day to the damp and the shadows of Robin's Nest. Depressed, I moved from room to room. Visions of you, Rob, flitted through my mind like pictures extracted from the ever-changing shapes of wind-blown clouds. At last, desperate for some kind of human contact, I turned to my shrine, to the tiny treasure chest on the fireplace mantel with the letter inside: found its key, turned the latch, raised the smooth domed lid of the handmade box, one step at a time.

A soft tune escaped, a Brahm's serenade, like a sigh from the past. Removing the letter, unfolding its pages, I heard the sweet notes dance above the muffled cascade of the water outside. Focusing, I paused — the letter, I had realized abruptly, was upside down. Righting it, I was amazed when the words *Dear Son* leapt out from the page, for with them there arose a vivid recollection of my father's living hands: slender, tapered, clean but calloused, the hands of the expert shaver, the music box maker, only then, instead of a hammer or razor, they held paper and pen, caught in the midst of shaping two simple words of affectionate address — *Dear Son . . .*

My own hands collapsed. Tears burned my eyes. As if a cruel joke, as I tossed my head from side to side, I absorbed the message of the PLAN AHEad sign. Lonely for you, Rob, I finally understood. Understood not just abstractly but in the beat of my blood, with a father's desperate love, how he must have felt, that young second lieutenant all those miles away from home, apart from his son and surrounded by death. I knew, because I'd been made to feel it too, the compulsion behind his inadequate words, the need to connect; knew then, as the rain came down and the music

61

softly played and my hip pressed against the cold gray stone of the fireplace, that it was to you most of all that I owed an explanation for my reckless escape.

And so the idea was given to me, an unexpected legacy. From father to son to father to son — after all this confusion, after all this meandering as if aping the Inspector's story-telling method, we come to A.1. For just as my father engendered me, *his* letter engendered *this* letter; his attempt to explain and connect, this attempt. Now I know that the parallel isn't perfect, isn't just. I know that I wasn't drafted, that I'm not at war defending democracy against the Nazis. I recognize all too clearly that there's nothing so heroic or noble about my exile here. But I thought if I wrote you to tell you how much I missed you, if I gave you a document, my hand to your hand, a document which, however ineptly, might attempt to address my unexplained absence; I thought perhaps that on some distant day when you better understand the world as it is, how a bleak stockade of memos and garden hose, of scripted mornings and fathers-in-law can close a man in, then you might begin to grasp why it was that I had done what I had done — why I wasn't there.

And I thought, too, that I might in the process present to you the grandfather you never had — the mailman to offset the millionaire. I hoped through the letter to recover and express just exactly what it was which made him so special, the strange and yet wonderful father that he was. But now more than ever I remain confused. I try to remember a story, an image, some specific advice he might have given, but nothing by itself seems at all sufficient. Nothing quite evokes the full affect of the man himself, the way he made me feel by simply being in the house. The memories which haunt me most — like the morning shave, like the dazzle of his keys dangling from the chair — would, I suspect, seem inconsequential to someone else. Although I want to make you feel the way he made me feel, what I keep on hearing in the quiet of the pond and in the stillness of the store is the spectral sound of my father's singing. And that, I'm afraid, I can't reproduce.

On the beach of the past, there are tracks but not the man — symbols, half-abstract. Memories can be transformed by the tide of the years, worn smooth, obscured, like beaded bits of glass. I remember now the rare sound of his laugh. I remember, a timeless image, the way he would touch the pieces of wood he purchased, an exploration which became a caress. (You should have seen, Rob, how the grain would emerge, come alive like stroked fur, when worked by his hands.) I remember the way he would grunt and nod above a fishing book or tool catalogue when, interrupting her monologue, my mother would periodically call his name. "Douglas?" she would say, worried, faintly frowning, in a kind of choral refrain, wanting to extract from him before she went on a simple sound to prove that he was there; and I wonder now if the source of that frown, if what my mother dimly sensed in those recurring silences, was some fleeting premonition of his early death.

Can you picture him, Rob, your grandfather — a tall gaunt man whose long legs and arms were deceptively strong, hardened by the mailman's route he walked? Would it help to tell you that his hair was kept short, that his clothes, although neat, were absurdly mismatched, worn in combinations like a flannel shirt, Bermuda shorts, Hush Puppy loafers with ankle-length socks, that I have yet to meet another man who combined such general fastidious-

63

ness with such disregard for the way he looked? Which feature might suggest the peculiar power of your grandfather's presence, his effect on strangers, the way his silence, unlike the silence of the merely shy, had an aura of unsettling authority?

Should I start with the eyes? Although small, they were of a blue so arrestingly bright that they call attention to themselves even in my mother's war-time photos with their pedestrian palette of blacks and whites. And when they stared, those eyes remained uncannily still; blazing, they seemed, in their intensity, to see straight through. Even friends, when pinned by his silent gaze, would fidget and squirm, sneak glances at their clothes trying to discern if something were wrong, wondering uncomfortably just exactly what it was — a spot on a shirt? an unzipped fly? the self-deception about which they had constructed their lives? — my father was seeing with those see-through eyes.

I wondered, too — wonder still. When he first came home from the war, this gaunt immense stranger with the penetrating eyes, I shied away, terror-stricken, assuming that his stares and his silence were a form of censure. I would actually stiffen when he neared, on the verge of a flinch, anticipating, in the awful stillness of his presence, an eruption of rage directed toward me. But the eruption never came. Starved of evidence, the terror I felt began to wither away, replaced by acceptance, by a tentative affection, gratitude that I had at last been given a companion, someone whose silence, although intimidating, could also be a refuge, a haven from my mother's exhausting theatrics. Actions replaced words. He did the things a father should. He took me to the park; he made me toys out of wood; when I was sick, he was there by my bed, his composure a reassuring antidote to my mother's more panicky style of love. Day by day he earned his way, this late-arriving father, into my heart.

And yet something was wrong. Bypassing contentment, my attitude switched during those first six years from self-centered fear to compassionate concern; loving my father, I began to worry about him, as if I were a parent myself. Yes, something was wrong. Although all the parts were in place — a pretty and vivacious wife, an intelligent husband returned from the war, a "starter" house in the suburbs, a small two-story on the wrong side of the right kind of town — the dream machine refused to run. (Does the story begin to sound familiar, Rob?) I could hear it first in my mother's voice, the way her optimism turned shrill, almost hysterical, like a losing country's war propaganda, as my father bounced from job to job. I could see it, too, in my father's eyes — the pain exacted as he tried to adjust to a junior executive's vision of life.

And I saw something more. Once my terror of him passed, I began to sense as a child dimly senses, feelings stripped of causes, the all-abiding sadness which hid behind my father's silence. It was as if, scarred by the war, he had been forced to draw some final conclusion which killed all dreams before they are born. It was as if, with those severe and testing stares of his, he were searching for a reason to hope for more, searching within each man and woman he met for some missing piece of evidence which could prove that dark conclusion wrong. And when time after time he dropped that stare, glancing away as he always glanced away — smileless, wordless, apparently unchanged — I couldn't help but feel that we, the objects of his scrutiny, had somehow failed him; that given a chance

65

to tempt him back, we had instead driven him further into his exile. I didn't know what it was he saw in us then with those blazing see-through eyes of his. I only knew that what he saw made him sad.

The tension in our house grew. Another layoff or resignation, my father retreating more and more into the workshop he had built in our tiny basement, my mother more and more on the phone, plotting with her sister, my Aunt Delia, seeking in anxious, secretive, hesitant whispers for a strategy that would, like the May sun the Maine woods, rouse my father's dormant ambitions. They never argued in my presence; perhaps they never argued directly at all. The hushed misunderstanding, the unhappiness which suffused their marriage went unnamed, as if a conspiracy of silence could save them — and me — from the unwelcome truth. I knew, though, even I knew; not the facts but the feeling of that truth. His sadness and her panic met each day across the dinner table like the fronts of two contrasting weather systems — clouds of silence, dark horizons, a taste of ozone in the air.

I was scared, Rob, confused and scared. Like you perhaps on the day I left, when you cried in your crib, somehow sensing disaster in my goodbye kiss, I lived in dread of an approaching event whose actual shape I could not glimpse. Something was wrong, I knew only that and nothing more; something was wrong between my parents and it was up to me, I began to feel, an eight-year-old with adult-sized fears, to prevent that something from getting worse.

I made it my mission to preserve the peace. Diversion was the tactic I used, a constant effort to keep them pleased. Wanting to soothe my mother's panic, I became as "good" as I could, tried to conform to her highest standards. Wanting to cajole my father out of his sadness, I took to telling jokes, stupid, silly, grammar school jokes whose predictable punch lines assaulted the ear like my toy violin's dissonant notes. I was desperate. I was relentless. What I lacked in subtlety, I made up with persistence. Rushing home from school, I would refuse to leave my parents alone in a room, playing instead the nervous chatty chaperone, talking in their presence more and more, hoping apparently, in a vague imitation of my mother's style, to mask their despair with my endless noise.

It was a pathetic and, in the end, self-defeating campaign. With my anxious glances and hyper chatter, with my habit of diving atop their every spoken phrase as if it were a hurled grenade, I only magnified the tension in the air; lit up, like a phosphorescent flare, the very conflict I was trying to conceal. The conspiracy of silence became harder to sustain. The siege of my inept diplomacy put pressure on us all, day after day, until — unable to bear it and worried, I suspect, by my odd behavior — my father chose to end the stalemate.

"I start on Monday," he said. They were the first words I heard that day when I entered the house, and there was something about the way they were pronounced, a weariness about the edges, a resigned impatience, that hinted of repetition, of an argument going round and round.

"You can't," my mother said.

There was a pause. Freezing in the doorway, I let my schoolbooks slip with a muffled thud to the carpeted floor: I seemed to know with that one brief exchange that my

67

desperate peacekeeping mission had failed, that the unknown event which I'd feared for so long and been scrambling to prevent had, in my absence, already taken place.

"Hello?" I called out, in the doorway still — I was hoping that my presence, once known, would enforce a truce. They were in the kitchen, though, and my tentative voice hadn't broken through.

"Is there something wrong?" my mother asked. "Are you ill? Are you doing this to punish me, is that what it's about? Is it some kind of joke?"

"It's what I want to do."

"Want to do? . . . People don't want to do that. They may *have* to, but they don't *want* to; they don't *choose* —"

"Hello!" I called out again. In the brief silence that followed, forgetting to shut the outside door behind me, I rushed across the living room. As I approached the kitchen, their reemerging voices dropped to a whisper and the pace of the dispute suddenly quickened.

"You could talk to Teddy."

"I don't want to talk to Teddy."

"He'd be glad to help."

"I don't want help, Lil."

"He'd know where to send you — you know he would."

"I'm home, Mom," I said, arriving at last at the door of the room.

"*You know he would,*" she hissed, leaning toward him, one last furious assertion. Reaching down then, she tried to hide beneath her hand a letter lying on the table beside her.

"I'm home."

There was a pause. I was ignored. My mother stared at my father who stared to the floor; I stared at the letter

68

partially concealed by my mother's palm. The kitchen was small, more a submarine's galley than an actual room, another challenge to my mother who tried to offset its claustrophobic gloom with a tropical decor, all oranges and yellows, a lemon-colored phone hanging on the wall where it waited to be plucked, hand to hungry mouth, like a ripe piece of fruit; and within its close bright space, our family of three was squeezed into place, unable to move.

"Douglas?" my mother finally said. (How many times did I hear her call his name like that, trying, always trying, as if a gypsy at a seance, to lure him back?)

"Yes."

"You're not doing this, Douglas. You are not doing this."

Doing what? I wanted to know but, afraid of the answer, refused to ask. Like the jaws of a compactor, her hand on the table was slowly contracting — crushing, ingesting the letter it hid.

"I am, Lil."

"I'll call Delia, that's what I'll do — I'll call Delia and Teddy. They could be here in an hour; we'll have them over for dinner . . ."

"Mom?" I quickly said: there was something about the smile bedizening her face, slightly off-center like a cheap toupee, which had filled me with dread. My father meanwhile, a hand to his brow, was slumping against a counter and shaking his head.

". . . We'll have them over for dinner. There's a steak, I think, one steak in the freezer. A London broil — it should be enough to feed them. I can cook some pearl onions, we'll make Brandy Alexanders. You and Teddy can talk after dinner —"

"It won't do, Lil."

"Of course it will. It was nearly two pounds, I saw it in the freezer. I bought it on sale. It'll be enough to feed them."

"It won't do. I can't be what you want me to."

My mother blinked, reared back; seemed suddenly, as if through the assertion of superior breeding, to remove herself from the argument. "I don't believe this, I really don't believe this," she said to the wall, to the phone, as if she were plotting with Delia when my father wasn't home, as if she were complaining to the author of a scene in which she'd been performing against her will. But the illusion of escape didn't last long; turning back, distraught, she attempted to probe — pleaded almost — for an excusable cause.

"Is there something wrong? Are you ill? Would you like to see the minister or Dr. Jones?"

"Mom? . . . Dad?"

"Are you sick, is that it? Is there something else that I ought to know?"

"Monday," my father said, beginning again, wearily, wearily shaking his head. (This was where I came in. I could feel a draft from the door I'd left open chill the back of my legs. Pleading for attention, I began to pull on a pleat of my mother's dress.) "I start on Monday."

"You can't."

"Mom?"

"Do you hear me, Doug?"

"Listen to me, Mom —"

"You can't, you can't, you can't," she said.

"*What is it, damn it?*" she suddenly added, whirling in my direction, wrenching away the hand which, with ever-

70

increasing urgency, as if clutching the rip cord to a para-chute, had been yanking on her dress. And she turned on me so fast, her voice was so harsh, her expression so intense, her grip on my wrist so unexpectedly painful, her tear-shaped nails raking my skin; it seemed so crucial to smooth things over, to succeed *at that very moment* in somehow making them happy again — that I was at a loss what to say. All that came to mind in the panic of my silence was another of my jokes, a juvenile riddle whose punch line-answer I can no longer recall.

"Why is an elephant's tail so small?"

"Why what?" she said. Her posture sagged, her fea-tures softened, her head listed slightly as if the absurdity of my question had destabilized her sense of balance.

"Why is an elephant's tail so small?"

Repeated, my grammar school riddle unmoored her completely. She took a step back, releasing my hand, her mouth still open, her eyes glazing over. "Doug*las*?" she called out plaintively then, casting a disoriented gaze about the room, and it was as if she were lost or had suddenly gone blind, seeking in my father's voice a familiar land-mark, a signpost to guide her through the terrain of the moment, its earthquake rubble, this catastrophe which had become her life.

For a long moment there was no reply. Hot air, escap-ing from a vent, rippled the hem of my mother's dress and pressed the tablecloth against her thigh. The letter she had hidden, as if an improvised toy for a playful kitten, had been crumpled into a ball; it lay where it had fallen, unshielded, now forgotten, a wad of words on the bright tile floor. Dad's eyes found mine. They were not blazing, they did not

search me; they seemed to accept, without the usual prob-
ing, the inevitability of disappointment: no, I could not
check his sad conclusion.

"You better go to your room," he told me.

. . . Can you see it, Rob: the mother, the father, the son,
the bright tiny room, that claustrophobic caldron of our
familyhood? Will my word-picture do? Can I write to you in
the space command center of our Colton Falls kitchen, with
its island counter, its eye-level broilers, with its frost-free
refrigerator with spigot for ice water; write to you there
from the kitchen I rent in Johnson Mills about the kitchen
we shared in my childhood house and somehow expect to
approximate the truth? Here, in Robin's Nest, the burners
on the propane stove must be lit by a match. There's a hole
in the wide-planked floor which must be covered with a
brick or the chipmunks will sneak in and raze the trash.
Alone, I have a tendency to eat too fast. Food and solitude, I
find, do not mix. The rhythm is all wrong; without another
human face or voice, there is no natural reason to pause.
Hesitations, fork in hand, seem too posed — phony, artificial, like the smiles I would wear when Marjorie's father
was in the house. In part, Rob, it's because I worry so much
about *his* influence that I'm struggling to resurrect for you
now an alternative — the grandfather you never had.

The mother, the father, the son, the bright tiny room.
The wad of words, a notice from the postal service, crumpled on the floor. Examining them now as I might an old
maple leaf, its color worn away, a fragile fossil-like design, a
network of veins, left in its place, I can see how our life
together was irrevocably changed; how our peculiar pattern, our morphology as family, was fixed that day. And I
can gauge now, too, my mother's reaction; can imagine,

72

with a grown man's compassion, as I turn that leaf slowly in my hand, trying to do justice to every angle, how she must have felt as she stood there between my father and myself, stunned into silence by my ridiculous joke.

Meant to amuse her, my question had, instead, become the final emblem of her profound confusion. She had that day lost her vision of the future — not just her son, but her husband, her marriage now posed a riddle which she could not answer. And as she glanced about the room with its brightly painted walls and lemon-colored phone, enclosed in the fist of its gaudy decor, as she fixed once again her exact position according to her own compass of achievement and acquisition, her confusion gave way to what I recognize today as an expression of horror. This, *this* was the prospect she now glimpsed before her. As it was, it would be. What she had secretly feared, she now, after my father's announcement, had come to believe: that despite her ambitions she might always be trapped in a galley-size kitchen; that her "starter" home might be her final home, that she was destined to remain a suburban prole — a coupon clipper, the luckless sister. One who would always be found where she stood right now: on the wrong side of the right kind of town.

The alternative, though, was Little Chester. The alternative was Rockwell Speedway, potluck suppers, vegetable gardens that were not hobbies; the "high society" of Methodist women meeting to plan a cookie sale, proceeds to rebind spine-snapped hymnals — for her, a fate as severe, an exile just as punishing as my father's projected promotion to the executive suite.

The stalemate hadn't ended; it had been defined. The announcement had revealed with devastating clarity the contradiction which lay at the center of their lives, how each was drawn to what the other would find a humiliating environment. It had revealed to my mother what my father had already recognized: that the status quo which they both disliked, that their life in this house, in this town, amended only by my father's mailman job — *that the stalement itself* — could be the only possible compromise. They would have to stay where they were, neither city nor country, neither rich nor poor, trapped in this subdivision limbo between his dreams and hers; they would have to accept this sphere of limited mutual unhappiness or risk the prospect of something worse: endless fights, the trauma of divorce.

(Why, I ask myself now as I patrol the store or stare across the pond, as I strike a wooden match above my propane stove, why couldn't Marjorie and I negotiate a compromise? Is it because I refused to reenact the intricate dance of assertion and concession, of heroic endurance and self-deception which dominated my parents' lives? Is it because I wanted more, and more is too much? Could it be that all marriages which last are merely spheres of limited mutual unhappiness — bargains struck against the dark? Every couple, when examined, seems to me now an unlikely pairing. My aunt and uncle. My parents. The powerful Marie and Chief Inspector. Even the mill hands and their wives — they tend to shop at different times and I'm always wrong when I try to match them in my mind, try to guess from what they say and how they dress, from the items on their shopping lists, who has chosen whom for life. Is it best to be different or alike? to be like brother and sister, have the same values, background, expectations or, as my parents did, achieve a subtle balance of opposing

74

interests? I'm curious, for example, about my boss's marriage, about the mysterious, unseen Mrs. Chapman. [Should I call her *Mrs.* Bob, I wonder?] Does she actually exist? Does she, as I've come to imagine, also never have to raise her voice? Does she, as I want to believe, like Mr. Bob and the Chapman kids, have the same red hair, the same wide forehead and narrow chin, the same dark green eyes which rarely blink — cloned not just by genes but by geography, some moral ether in the air they breathe? Marjorie changed. She grew more like her father day by day, as if the years we had spent together, college and after, were only a phase, the humble cocoon from which inevitably emerged this extravagant creature, Rich Man's Daughter, who could only be sustained on the nectar of orchids. Perhaps, as in the past, marriages should be arranged. Committees formed to study family trees, to chart habits, histories, subtle genetic tendencies. To test, for incompatibility, samples of the home-town soil.)

My parents' marriage survived — an unlikely hybrid of the unalike. Gradually, a rhythm returned to our family life: no more awful jokes, fewer tense stares across the dinner table; just mother, father, and only son assuming a pattern beguilingly similar to the one they had followed long before that landmark fight.

This semblance of continuity required effort. Confronted with the truth, Mom worked to suppress it. Evolving a strategy of self-deception which was aided by my father's silence, she never discussed his mailman's job and took to rising late so she wouldn't have to face the ignominious donning of his uniform — that literal blue collar her husband wore. Thus shielded, her own secret censor, as safe from reality as the Chief Inspector, she could pretend to herself that nothing had changed, that our station in life was still temporary; she could return to her hopes, her schemes, her skull sessions with sister Delia, her indefatigable redecorations. She still insisted, as if I were an exiled prince, that I learn the niceties of etiquette. She still listened to public radio (free, of course), still arranged cut flowers (grown herself), still kept up with the latest books (borrowed, not bought, from friends and from the library); she still dressed each evening as if important guests — those mysterious "connections" my father and I never seemed to make — just might be dropping by for dinner. As before, she used my father's silence like a blank screen onto which she could project her uncontested fantasies; but now, chastened by the truth, secretly aware that if pushed again he'd tell her again "It won't do, Lil. I can't be what you want me to," she was careful to avoid a confrontation.

Occasionally, though, when a friend's husband was promoted or when some acquaintance was found to be moving to a more prestigious neighborhood, the contrast between wishes and facts would be too glaring to dismiss and her illusion of hope would temporarily collapse. She would turn morose, distraught. Appearances would be neglected, her wardrobe reduced to a bathrobe and slippers; the house would be ignored — dinners uncooked, beds unmade, dahlias left to rot in their vases. Eventually the letter would appear, performed to our embarrassment and climaxed with tears. Or, rarer, she would make another attempt to convert my father: plot with Delia, invite her and Teddy to our house for dinner where, over pearl onions and Brandy Alexanders and the special steak which always seemed to have been stored away for just this purpose,

Uncle Teddy would, once again, fail to lure my father out of the blue and gray of the postal service.

Afterward, my parents would fight. These arguments, however, repeated over long intervals, grew increasingly predictable, less threats to stability than rituals of renewal; like children threatening to run away from home, their paths always looped back to the same safe conclusion. To the status quo. To his silence and her false hope. To the terms of their tacit compromise.

Dad, too, had to sacrifice to meet the terms of that compromise, although as befit his personality, his was a steadier submission, a quiet, uncomplaining acceptance of limits. Suburban Connecticut, my mother's dinner parties, her ceaseless campaign to improve, to enrich us, these he all bore with the same stoicism, refusing both to protest or to pretend enjoyment, drawing sustenance instead from those two private passions, fishing and woodworking, which were the legacy of Little Chester — a bit of Maine, like a pine sachet, which he carried with him.

Whenever he could, on weekday nights and weekend mornings, after he had fulfilled his obligations as father, husband, postal worker, he would escape down the stairs to his basement workshop where, among his fishing gear and music boxes, he would lose himself in his latest project. The total time subtracted from his week was small, but when I try now to understand the self-sacrificial life he led, how he managed to survive all those years in a subdivison in Connecticut, what comes to mind first is the punctuating click of that cellar door's latch, the sound of his feet on those hollow wooden steps; what I recall most of all are those brief retreats beneath the ground, for they seem somehow to capture him best: how he withdrew, always withdrew, from the world into his house, from his house into his room, from others into himself — an island of self-sufficiency in a sea of enrichment; how he required the refuge of a private cell, a place where he could practice, without needless explanations, his craftsman's vision of refinement and precision, and within which, perhaps, he hoped to create on a smaller scale an order of things more perfectly made — model worlds immune to the sadness he found at the top of the stairs.

A peculiarity of the house, we could often overhear him as he worked. His bench was near the furnace and the sounds of his tools — the rasp of a saw, the rhythmic stripping stroke of a plane, the *tap-tap-tap* of a finishing hammer driving home a decorative nail — would be absorbed and passed on, funneled telephonically through the arterial system of heating ducts. They would rise with the heat to the end of each line where, disembodied, softened by their passage and slightly distorted, they would seep like dreams through the grills of the vents into the sleeping body of the house, haunting as they spread its every numb limb, every last darkened room . . . even mine, the most distant of all, on the second floor.

It was an otherworldly and yet oddly reassuring experience, eavesdropping on my father through the accidental intercom, absorbing, unseen, the music he made with hammer and saw. As I lay in bed, afraid of the dark, worrying about school or my parents, the multiform mystery of growing up, as I pressed to the edge of the mattress nearest the vent, drawn like a light-seeking moth to those muffled sounds of his craftsmanship, I felt less alone — I felt like a shipwreck survivor on a deserted island who had caught at last, through star-bursts of static, a voice in the night on his radio. And like a shipwreck survivor, I wanted to imagine that that voice was meant for me. I liked to believe that my father knew I was listening, that this was, in fact, his secret way of contacting me, that reduced to the elements of self which mattered to him most — the skill, the patience, the care it took to make something well — he was speaking to me then in his truest voice, the only one he could trust, passing on to me then, through those coded sounds of tools shaping wood, all the wisdom he couldn't put into words. All the unspoken love.

And so I listened, son at the knee of the invisible father. Lying on the edge of my bed, feeling the heat rise from the open vent as if Dad's own breath against my face, I listened to his secret message. And listening, I forgot — forgot tomorrow's uncertainties and my fear of the dark; forgot even, in the very midst of struggling to comprehend it, the sadness behind my father's eyes. The room would grow warm, my pillowcase hot; the hand which had been clutching a blanket up to my chin would go gradually limp and drop over the side, dangling there above the floor. From the depths of the basement, soft sounds would emerge. A mallet's rap. A drill's churning. The muffled clap of a vise closing. Sandpaper of the finest gauge would abrade the silence subtly, smoothing the coarser grain of my thoughts. Sometimes, as I drifted off to sleep, wrapped in that aura of warmth and peace, I could hear him talk. I'd hear him say beneath his breath as if a conductor pleading with his instruments, "Fit now," or "Don't split on me"; overhear him murmur urgently, "That's it, that's it," as he coaxed cut pieces into place. Sometimes there would be a pause, as if he had stopped to judge the harmonious whole his care had wrought; a satisfied sigh, like a sentry's "All's well!", might then float up through the heating ducts and into the house — all would grow still. Sometimes, Rob, as I lay there in the dark, floors apart, I could hear my father sing to himself.

Can you imagine it: those late nights and early mornings, the dark of my room, my face to the wall, drifting off to sleep beside the vent, buoyed within its womb of warmth and sound? Can you possibly sense the reassurance and relief, the intoxicating peace I felt on those rare rare nights when I caught from afar the muted fragments of my father's song? I'm afraid that you can't. There are moments, Rob, when I doubt my ability to revive for you even the vaguest glimpse of the life I've led, when I begin to believe that we all live alone and apart, in separate cabins on separate ponds whose separate seasons cannot be shared. And yet if our stories can't be told, our experience passed on, what, I wonder, are fathers for?

The mother, the father, the only son; that familiar voice, balanced somewhere between resignation and concern, suggesting that I retreat to my room . . . I keep glancing back. I keep turning, turning that leaf in my hand. Despite my doubts, I keep trying to rescue the present with the past, hoping that with one more detail recalled, with a slightly different slant, my family's pattern will be fixed and I'll understand: know who I was, who I am, know the kind of man I should become when I emerge from my stay at Robin's Nest.

The tablecloth, I recall, was a yellow print. My mother, elegant even then in a homemade, calf-length cranberry dress, wore a string of artificial pearls around her neck; her fingers touched them lightly as she stared into space, as if touching for the last time the cold folded hands of a loved one deceased. Dad, forlorn, stared at me from across the room; unable to move, his figure was obscured, the narrow passage blocked, by my mother's stunned and motionless form. So silent, so still, and yet even this, our fixed positions, seemed to express an underlying truth. For, in a way, she was always in the center, always between us — this woman who had known us both first, who had introduced us. Her words, her tears, her crises, her ambitions, her oversized loves and fears, her anguished readings of my father's letter; even in her absence, she managed to affect us: habituated to our silent roles, we rarely spoke; instead, glanced at each other with shy, affectionate surprise, like fellow members of an audience exchanging mute hellos from across an aisle.

That afternoon, however, we exchanged mute goodbyes. Turning away from their inexplicable scene, from the crumpled letter and my mother's catatonic stare, I took my father's advice: backed away, crossed the floor, closed the open front door, bent down to retrieve the books I had dropped, pausing there in a state of shock, frightened, though, too that they'd renew their fight. The air by the door and the smooth plastic covers of the books I had dropped were chilled. From the kitchen, breaking the silence, I heard the phone's metal cradle snap up and then my father's voice, gently attempting to rouse a response — "Lil?" — but the sound of the dial was the only reply. There was an uneasy pause. Afraid to move and call attention to myself, I remained where I was. Grimacing, I took a step closer when I heard the high pitch of desperation in my mother's voice.

"Delia? It's me, Dee, it's me. Thank God you're home.

81

You won't believe . . ." Her voice broke and she was forced to stop; her sister's name, when it emerged again, was less spoken than sobbed. "Dee? You just won't believe it, Dee — you won't."

What wouldn't she believe, I wanted to know; but just then, as I took another step closer, the kitchen door swung shut, cutting me off.

It seemed sometimes that all of childhood was a banishment like that, trapped alone on the wrong side of a closed door, adult voices dimly overheard but too obscured to understand. And later, after Delia and Teddy made their emergency appearance, after the meager dinner was served, Mom forced to decorate her plate with but a single thin slice of London broil, I was banished again — only this time my mother was the one, firmly backed up by my conspiring aunt, who directed me to go to my room.

The pattern was being set that night, all these steps to be ritualized: the fight, the S.O.S. call to my aunt, the steak taken from the freezer, the strained innocuous dinner conversation, the boy sent to his room, the adults, too, retreating to their specified stations — Mom and Delia huddling in the kitchen while Teddy, their assigned representative, reluctant apostle of the careerist ethic, made his foredoomed attempt to convert my father. Yes, the pattern was being set, but it did not seem like a pattern yet. I had no sense at all of what might happen next. Instead, everything seemed so new, so strange, so indefinably dangerous, an undercurrent of emotion cascading beneath the conversation. Repetition alone, familiarity over time, would dilute the sense of threat I felt as, toying with my food, I watched my family at the dinner table: Teddy's anxious smiles; Mom's hysterical chatter; Delia's hostile stares, sudden silent accusations, cast like darts in the direction of my father. I kept glancing back as I made my reluctant trek away from the table, as if at a swaying bridge I was afraid might collapse at any moment.

I didn't, as ordered, stay in my room. Too anxious to sleep, I snuck back down and hid myself near the foot of the stairs, a risky but strategic spot where I could, if I strained, my cheeks pressing against the railing, overhear bits of both conversations: to my left, the urgent whispers of the confiding sisters, their voices, like their taste in clothes and the values they held, so essentially similar that it was difficult to tell who was speaking; to my right, Uncle Teddy's voice alone, apparently forced by my father's silence into an uneasy, false-hearty monologue. Family voices. Familiar voices. Voices hurt, resentful, anger-charged, and caught in a haphazard fading counterpoint, like snatches of tunes playing on the radios of passing cars.

"He will." "Of course, he will." "Counseling," "it's perverse," "if you'd only give yourself half a chance," "the future," "the future," "the future" slipping out like a saint's sacred name from everyone's lips. "It's important at this stage that you position yourself . . ." I heard Teddy say — later, he laughed. "He never was the same," Delia complained, "after he came back." A table was slapped. My mother began to sob. Teddy laughed again, at his own joke I seemed to know without knowing why. "We're finished," Mom said, " — he might as well have put a gun to our heads." And then, even worse, binding me even closer to the mystery of the moment, that fear I would hear for the rest of my life: "he'll turn out just like him — I know he will."

(Was I the *he*? And what did that mean? That I, too

would be sad? That I, too, would "catch" whatever it was my father had caught; be the cause, the source, of these inexplicable sobs?)

It was all so confusing, the two conversations, the half-heard phrases, the elliptical allusions, the sobs from the kitchen and Teddy's laughter. The more I overheard, the less I understood. The longer I remained there, the closer I drew to the bottom of the stairs until, almost in view and hearing the chairs scrape against the kitchen tile, I was forced to rush back up to my distant room. There, the voices were dimmer still. Minutes passed before I heard Uncle Teddy's bellowed goodbye and a muffled thud as the front door closed. Drawn like a witness whose duty it was to note every twitch of an execution, I watched from my window as their car backed out; traced its slow retreat from my secret, second-story sentry post until its wedge of soft light was extinguished by the dark — and with it, I felt, some final fragile reason to hope.

Alone, all alone in my room. The silence so complete that it was easy to believe that my parents had gone too, the ghost of their unhappiness left behind, a gray tinge to the light, to haunt the house. What did *I* know? About marriage, about ambition, about the secret fallibility of parents, about the scars of war and the love of sisters? All these clues, somehow both too many and too few, glimpses of a crisis beyond an eight-year-old's limited sphere of comprehension. My mother's stunned stare, my father's "It won't do," her pleas to make an appointment with Dr. Jones. Teddy and Delia arriving at the house. "You better go to your room," Dad said as if he already knew what was in store for him — my mother's sobs and Teddy's soft sell. Banished to my room.

84

Shadows from the leafless trees outside the house dipped and swayed across the ceiling; as if a projected slide of my state of mind, they sustained their restless, ceaseless, trackless motion — an intricate maze without solution. No way out. No answers, no escape, trapped in this tiny, half-lit, silent space which had been squeezed into an almost tepee shape by the slope of the roof. My made bed, my cleared desk, my bureau drawers flush against their frame, every article of clothing put away — all part of my pathetic campaign to prevent the fight which, utterly indifferent to my good behavior, had just taken place: why couldn't the thoughts in my mind, my parents' lives, be so neatly arranged?

Inevitably, I misunderstood. A boy, with a boy's fears, a boy's impoverished experience, I drew a boy's fantastic and frightened conclusions as I lay awake in my room beneath those shadows trying to make sense of all the clues. (What fantastic conclusions you drew, Rob, what misunderstandings formed in your just-forming mind when you overheard your parents fight; what conclusions you draw now about the father who ran out when you hear him attacked by his bitter wife — I'm afraid to ask.) My father was ill; there was something terribly, terribly wrong with him, I was sure. Some slow-working disease, some hidden, debilitating injury: cancer, craziness, some condition which, like the whisperings of sex, like the glaze on my grandfather's eyes the day before his death, evoked a force beyond my capacity to name. A wound from the war; a bit of baneful shrapnel radiating its poison cell by cell, day by day from the center of his gut. Something subtle and strange, the source of the fever behind his sky blue stare, the force that took the words away — all the comfort and advice that would have

85

been mine if he hadn't been stripped of his capacity to speak. Something final. Something furtively strong. Something, too, like a hemophiliac's propensity to bruise, which could be passed on: mine to suffer too in the years to come.

He would die, he would leave, my parents would divorce; anonymous men — doctors, soldiers — would remove him from the house, the sound of boots on the stairs, diseases named behind closed doors. He would disappear: at once, atomized in his chair, my mother glancing up from her monologue, perpetually, futilely calling his name; or withdraw by degrees, his silence now but the initial stage of some irreversible quarantine, first his voice, then his legs, then his arms, then his fine-boned hands slowly erased, until, like the cartoon animals at the Saturday matinee, only the eyes were left behind, a faceless stare floating in space, their furious blue searching still for the missing piece of evidence, that clue which could prove his sadness wrong.

In the dark, fear gained weight; possibilities turned into intractable beliefs. Causes could shift and mix like the silhouetted branches above my head, but the results, I was sure, would remain the same: separation, loss—something so much more final and severe than a simple change in jobs. Because my father had always seemed so sad, because he *hadn't* been with me for my first year-and-a-half, it was too easy, too terrifyingly easy as I lay there then, alone in my room, to imagine him gone. His absence would be the loneliness of that very moment extended on and on and on and on. The man who faithfully came to all my games, who took me to the park; the parent who, because he was calmer, accompanied me to all the major transitions of my life—doctor visits, the first day of school—who ushered me through the most frequent and frightening transition of all,

86

easing me awake with a knock on my door ("Another day," he would sometimes say without the slightest hint of either hope or despair—I can hear it even now). The man with the surgeon's hands; the man of quiet good sense; the man who suffered with me when the letter was read, who had become a fellow member of the audience, my silent sharer across the aisle; *that* man . . . *him* . . . my late-arriving friend: gone from my life. Gone again.

I squirmed in my bed, memories of my father swirling through my head, guilt pressing itself like a leaden quilt against my ribs. All the danger I sensed, all the allegiance I felt, all the help I should but could not give: more than ever I felt that I had let him down.

The shadows, ever-changing webs of chaos, swept back and forth across the ceiling. My right cheek ached where, oblivious to all but my need to know, I had pressed too hard against the stairway railing. Damp palms and shallow breaths. The mute mockery of my meticulous desk. I pulled the covers off, then on, then off again, my heart fluttering and fast as if a rabbit grasped in unfamiliar hands, as if only moments before I had made my escape from the foot of the stairs—but hours had passed. Gradually, weighted with exhaustion, my arms went limp. Gradually, the room itself fading in and out of consciousness, I slipped into the realm of a dubious sleep: body dead, eyes half-open, mind still spinning, a cacophony of replayed voices. *"It won't do, Lil."/"He'll turn out just like him—I know he will."/"I can't be what you want me to."/"Doug-las? Where are you, Douglas?"/"The future, the future, the future,"* chanted over and over, an obnoxious chorus, as if the advertising jingle for a useless product./*"Where are you, Doug?"* . . .

87

The voices slowed, slurred; they disappeared and then reemerged. Borders blurred—ceiling with self, images with images, the objects of the room with the figments of memory—until, tiring, I began to lag behind my mind's ceaseless cascade of busyness and noise. I had no choice, no will. After a time, lost in some trackless region of the night, I seemed to be falling away from myself; seemed to sink, as if down the shaft of an endless well, away from an ever-narrowing circle of light whose circumference enclosed the sphere of my thoughts. And from that circle, someone watched. A face, which I understood to be my father's, peered over the edge and kept vigil over my slow collapse. A face familiar and yet frightening, less a snapshot than a cartoon drawing, its symmetry marred by a subtle addition: a small patch of beard—dark, tear-shaped, set like a tuft of sun-scorched moss in the hollow of his cheek—which my father had unaccountably forgotten to shave.

Its presence there unnerved me. I wanted to erase it. That he had missed those whiskers, that he had allowed this lapse in his usual standards as if forced to shave without a mirror, seemed an ominous act of carelessness, the shadow of some future danger. And although I couldn't be sure what the danger was, I felt I should warn him; it seemed imperative then as I continued to fall, watching my father watch myself, that I let him know that he wasn't finished, that a spot had been missed, that there was a flaw in his usually flawless craftsmanship and that until it was corrected he wouldn't be safe.

I pointed, but he didn't seem to see. The borders blurred again and it soon ceased to be clear, as that circle of light continued to recede, if I were falling from him or he from me. Panicking, I knew that I must not let him disappear; knew then that to let him go unwarned, the spot unshaved, was to banish him to some netherworld beyond my reach; knew then, with a terrifying certainty, that once he was gone, like those fathers who hadn't come back from the war, he would never again be allowed to return—not even a letter sent this time, from behind the lines, to take his place.

I tried to shout, strained to warn my father and rouse myself, but the words, trapped like stones in the rattle of my skull, wouldn't come out. It was as if the route had been severed from brain to mouth; as if, as my mother feared, I had already succumbed to my father's disease, his silence and solitude bearing me away, the circle of light meanwhile beginning to fade, smaller and smaller, dimmer and dimmer, until, reduced to just a luminous blur on the periphery of vision, its features blurred and I could no longer discern my father's face. (*Douglas? . . .Where are you, Douglas? . . . Where are you, Dad?*) Desperate, I squinted as if an act of attention might bring him back. Desperate to brake the fall, I struggled to escape my sleep-induced paralysis; tried to stir a leg, an arm, to lift a hand—but it seemed that I had forgotten how to move and would have to rediscover on my own, by chance, within my backbone's intricate maze of nerves, the one correct connecting path.

My plummet gained speed. The dark closed in. I fought my collapse until, no strength left, no will to resist, too exhausted even to sustain my fear, I gave up abruptly and surrendered myself to the silent sleep of nothingness. And with that surrender, panic turned to bliss. Strangely, through the very act of capitulation, as if struggle had been the obstacle all along and I could only have what I wanted by ceasing to want, I gained a soothing sense of buoyancy then. To quit was to win. To die was to live. To fall was to float: amazed, I watched from within the vacuum of my will-lessness as my collapse was seen to reverse itself. As, with effortless ease, borne on a current of inexplicable peace, I rose through the dark toward my father's waiting face, rose higher and higher, that circle of light growing wider and wider until its luminous sphere seemed to span the horizon; brought closer and closer until my eyes, already open, suddenly focused and I found myself staring at a familiar pattern, a rectangular grid: the grill of the vent beside my bed.

I was cold. I was lying on my side. An arm was pinned beneath my ribs. My covers were thrown or kicked to the bottom of the bed, my legs ankle-deep beneath their pile. A few feet away, the grill of the vent was painted white, its parallel slats dividing itself into alternating strips of dark and light.

I was cold. My pinned arm ached but couldn't move. Numb from sleep and the winter night's chill, I seemed frozen in time, suspended there within the silvery grain of the predawn light as if within a translucent tomb of glacial ice—my blanket still bunched at the bottom of the bed, my arm still trapped beneath my side, drool seeping from my slackened lips, staining the fringe of the pillowcase, my free hand draped across my thigh. Even my eyes couldn't move; remained fixed, slow-blinking, on the slats of the grill. A minute must have passed before I could separate the realm of my dreams from the realm of the room, before I understood that the current of peace which had teased me out of sleep was, in fact, a gentle stream of sound and heat whose origin was outside myself. The basement workshop. The arterial system of heating ducts. The grill of the vent, the

90

sound slipping through. My father's own breath, his voice, his words, stretched and shaped into a tune. The background beat of his woodworking tools. A minute must have passed before the simple facts explained themselves: I was lying on my side, on my bed, just before dawn and my father was in the basement, singing as he worked.

Surprised, I listened. Muted, his song floated into the room, a miniature globe, a world of its own, like a delicately crafted paperweight scene sealed in glass and adrift with snow—peaceful, private, mine to observe but not to inhabit. Like that paperweight world, reduced in size but perfectly proportioned, its features clear and yet diminished, softened. You should have heard it, Rob, in the gray before dawn, that rare rare sound of my father's song. Not anguished, not ill, an unremarkable baritone unself-consciously expressing itself. Rising, falling, sliding its way over forgotten lyrics, forcing its way through the niceties of tune as if through the swinging doors of a frontier saloon, surging and then fading beneath the sound of the tools. You should have heard it. That unexpected triumph. That ordinary voice making its extraordinary leap out of the abyss of its usual silence.

Drawn, I listened, a willing captive, stunned, still, ever more attentive, poised on the very edge of the mattress. And as I listened, turning sounds into pictures, I envisioned my father as he worked in the basement; saw the rapt stare, the sawdust in his hair, the precise and graceful movements of his hands; saw the slow creation of the music box he made, the melding of its parts, its hinges and locks and dovetailed joints, the smooth surfaces and sinuous grain. Through the grill, I heard the wooden handle of his bench vise twirl. I heard his plane shave layer after layer from a piece of wood, strips that would fall like snipped blonde curls. Outside, I could hear the winter wind blow; all around me, heard timber joints groan as the first wave of heat spread through our home. Relentlessly, repetitiously, the lyrics of the song gently arose, Dad's soft words floating in the room like the flakes of snow in the paperweight's globe, the adversity of its storm magically transformed into a visual sort of lullaby — a promise of refuge for those inside.

My eyes began to drift. The shadows on the ceiling, busy still but paler now, no longer seemed a threat. Drawing effortless breaths, my body went limp, dissolved by a warm, suffusing sleepiness, my paralysis transformed from disease to reward — a miraculous, luxurious license to rest.

The night was over. I had broken through. My father's escape out of silence had set me free too. He had rescued me as a father should — and without knowing that he had, through the simple act of being there, that voice at the other end of the vent. To know that he could sing at all, if only when alone; to know that he had chosen to remain, hadn't run out or been taken away; to know above all that he'd still be there when the morning came, that in an hour or so there would be another soft knock on my bedroom door, another sure transition out of the dark — was to feel as I never had before the peace of trust, the perfect safety of another's unconditional love. It may seem strange to you, Rob, or just a sorry stab at an alibi, but it's true that I felt closest to my father when we were apart, most protected by him when I was alone in my room and listening to him sing through the open vent.

The years pass and I sleep alone again, sunk into the mildewed mattress at Robin's Nest. The years pass and sons become fathers, fathers become dead; peace becomes

92

elusive, not mine to receive but mine to give. In the natural order of things, responsibilities shift, and yet there are no ducts in the walls, no secret private conduits from Johnson Mills to Colton Falls, and I'm at a loss at how to provide for you a tranquillity I no longer possess.

I write instead. Against all odds, I try to turn this letter into a rough replacement for my father's song — something to clutch in the years to come when you, too, will lie alone in the dark wondering what it means to be a man. My words, you'll note if you read them then, keep turning to the past. Forgive me, Rob, if the comfort I offer is secondhand. I look to the memory of my father because he is all I have left, because I have no other choice. Because, saddened myself, I'm reduced to hoping now that if I tell my story well, if I succeed somehow in reviving for you the man himself and those nights we shared in my childhood house, then I just might succeed in reviving for us both the peace I would feel when eased into sleep by my father's voice.

And I wanted to provide something more — the one "something" which was missing when I was a boy. In those days of always tentative sanctuary, I liked to think, wanted to believe that Dad's silence was only temporary, that his withdrawal was but a chosen moral strategy, a protest against my mother and my aunt, part of the pact we shared against those who cheapened words by talking too much. I wanted to believe that a time would come when that self-imposed silence would suddenly end; a day when, having examined me for my readiness, he would pronounce me fit at last for apprenticeship, when he would take me down those stairs with him and there, among the hammers and planes and sandpaper, explain all the subtleties I didn't understand — the mysteries of marriage, the reason for

93

unhappiness, about God and sex and money and death, how it was possible to find within the relentless sadness of passing time a serenity which would not pass.

What I wanted then was words. What I wanted — *what I want* — was a second letter from him, one written after the death of his innocence, after the war. A letter which would transform his tacit wisdom into a voice, which would turn his reassuring presence into reassuring words, advice to recall whenever he was gone. A letter which, surviving his absence, could be read, reread, and then passed on. From hand to hand. From one boy to the next. From father to son to father to son.

But that letter never came; I never made that special journey down the cellar stairs. Dad's silence proved to be less a phase than a fate — if not a disease as my mother feared, then a destiny which defied escape. For as the years wore on, he continued to withdraw, a progressive recession into solitude whose pace only quickened after I left home. The fights with my mother became rarer and rarer. The boxes he made, as if his quest for perfection demanded an ever finer scale, grew smaller and smaller. Always a thin man, he became even thinner, as if he were undergoing a slow attrition, a self-abstention, a relentless retreat into the scarcity of winter. Until one day the progression was complete, perfection achieved, a silence without end, the fastidiously crafted flawlessness of death, and I was left behind then not only grieving but answerless.

And I'm answerless still. I confess, as I write to you now from my porch on the pond, while a solitary moth hurls itself again and again against the screen's fine mesh trying to reach the light inside, that I remain confused. It's a cloudy night here, cool and still. Mist has pooled above the shallow water and obscures the outermost tip of the

94

beached canoe. A cricket, hatched too late, sends out a tentative beacon of sound, searching the inlet for one of its own, for a mate it won't find, and it occurs to me slowly — an eerie, primitive, preverbal sort of knowing — that I recognize its song: the hesitancy, the lack of completion, the vague but enduring sensation that something is wrong, something missing.

Drawn, unable to write, I stare outside. The mist, the pond, a rotting log, the menacing blur of darkening forms: I cannot see far. The cricket's song ceases, an inrush of silence; and envisioning myself suddenly as if from a distance — how I float within the porch's small and fragile globe of light; how I'm just a speck, a photon's flash, a luminous mote within the universe, this wilderness of deepening darkness — I feel the panic of a man who awakes to the knowledge that he is going blind. An image of my mother rises in my mind, a memory from that day so many years ago now when she and my father had their fight. I see her go rigid, trapped in the kitchen. I see her stunned face, hear her lost voice, her call to my father for orientation. For an instant, it seems that I understand her completely. For a moment, it seems that I've come to feel the same awful premonition of failure; that I know what it means for the soul to shrink before the face of an inscrutable riddle.

No, I cannot see far. I want to guide you, Rob, but the sorry truth is that I have no map, that I've yet to find my own way out of the dark. I want to provide what I was missing, answers to rely on in your father's absence, but the sad fact is that I'm missing them still, that questions alone are all I can give you. What happened to my father when he fought in the war? What exactly was the sad conclusion that he seemed to have drawn? How is it possible to

95

surrender so much and yet remain so strong? How possible to raise a son when living with a woman you may no longer love, trapped in a marriage gone so wrong?

I would tell you if I knew. Please believe me when I say that I would sacrifice everything, my last chance for happiness, if I could just pass on to you that missing final word, the secret to it all. The answer seems near. I keep telling myself, perhaps because it is the only justification I have for running out, that I'm closer here in Maine, that a solution's at hand, that it lies somewhere within the mist above the pond, within the memory of the mother, father, and only son; that it lies just beyond reach, beyond sense; that it hides like the heron — here and yet not here, disguised by the nature of its perfect fit.

I do what I can, I persist. I watch, worry, reexamine, wait for another transfiguring event. I try to ignore the fact that the questions I ask, what I had hoped would be just a summer-long quest, seem to have no end. Like the moth whose futile striving sounds unnerve me now, I keep beating myself against the invisible screen of my ignorance: why are we here? why born to a world we're so ill-equipped to comprehend? why are we so sad so often? why do we have to be so lonely? why do we have to need so much and know so little, learn so slowly and die so soon? Why, Rob, do we have to die at all?

I stare outside, a mote within my tiny fragile globe of light. The mist, the pond, the obscured canoe. The encircling dark. The endless, chartless, unknown night. The oldest fear of all, the one my mother must have felt, tightening my throat.

"*Douglas*?" I want to call. Why, I want to ask him, why is an elephant's tail so small?

96

4.

Chapman's Yankee Trader, Rte. 45. The fall sun, listing toward the hills in mid-afternoon, casts its lemon-tinted light through the plate glass window, suspending the store in an illusion of stillness. No mill hands, no housewives, no children, no Chapman kids to help with dry goods. Mr. Bob, out of sight, counts fifths of gin in the liquor alcove. Calvin Wynn, out of sight, has planted himself in his usual position where, as mute and motionless as a cigar store Indian, he waits for the blast of the day shift's whistle. I stock scarves and gloves, stack rows on the shelves; I watch the way, as if ascending into space, particles of dust float slowly up the oblique streams of sunlight which immerse the aisle. Yes, the stillness is illusive. Time passes by even without people. The mill hums, dowels are cut, interest accrues in my father-in-law's trust fund accounts. In Connecticut, worrying, my mother ages; traveling east on Rte. 45, a school bus approaches the Yankee Trader, bearing the Chapman kid who'll be my replacement. Even in Johnson Mills, through the surreal golden light of an autumn afternoon, the mail is delivered. I would stop it all if I could, the bus, the rising dust, the sun above the hills : Marjorie's lawyer has sent me a letter.

In the alcove, bell-like, bottles rattle. I pause to take in the accidental music of gin, whiskey, muscatel. A Methodist, Mr. Bob doesn't drink himself, but he insists on each man's God-given right to earn his own way to hell. It's not the liquor that's bad, he explained to me once in another of those aphoristic nuggets which constellate his thought — it's the drunkard's abuse.

I smiled to myself then, silently adding the smugly wry observation: "And it's never good business to be holier-than-thou." But now, as I fold row after row of assorted scarves (plaid, fir green, a bright red even for hunters who want to safeguard their lives), the irony has given way to a country boy's fare of undisguised awe; given way, in the manner of his children, to deferential amazement at the phenomenon known as "Mr. Bob." For the truth is that my boss isn't holier-than-thou and yet still manages to believe what he believes without any evidence of doubt. How does it feel to know so well one's place in the world, to hold such a sure view? What must it be like to know — always, automatically — wrong from right, fixing as he does with those decimal-point eyes, precisely where one's own responsibilities lie?

Rows of scarves, stacks of gloves, bottles ringing in the alcove, the slow migration of rising dust . . . I'll be relieved by one of the Chapman kids (the boy, I think) at three o'clock. Ever since it arrived, I've wanted to show the letter to Mr. Bob. I've wanted to share it somehow, to pass the burden on to someone else. I've wanted to borrow from my boss's commonsensical view; wanted to ask him what the

98

letter actually means, what he thinks I should do. Has that allegorical cent already been lost, my last chance gone? Is it too late to go back now? What would *he* choose to say if he were writing one last letter to his only son? . . . More than ever, it seems, I need a wise father's advice.

Rows of scarves, stacks of gloves, empty boxes on the worn plank floor. It'll cost you ten-fifty this year to keep your neck warm. This much I know for sure: the lawyer forbids me to withdraw a single cent from our bank account (as if I would) — the price I pay for running out?

Even though I have trouble reading the letter, my mind freezing in panic, eyes skidding clumsily over the legalistic phrases as if an exam given in a foreign language, there's no doubt at all whose work it is, every line tatooed with my father-in-law's signature. Absurdly the man persists in believing, against all reason, because it fits the world as he chooses to misperceive it, that I married Marjorie to steal his millions. The surrender's complete — I should have known. He's taken charge again, I can see that now, Chairman of the Board back in Colton Falls, smothering Marjorie with his acquisitive love, managing her affairs with a tyrannically triumphant air of *I-your-father-told-you-so*. Bored since his retirement, he's found at last a project worthy of his special talent, that gift he has for a strategic application of bellicose passion. Suits, lawyer's threats, judicial injunctions: he'll go after me as if I were "the competition." I can picture him now, re-enthroned in his daughter's home, cursing on our phone, seething with a kind of rancorous joy as he arranges step by step, a cup of his favorite Turkish coffee throttled by the neck, my legal demise.

I know now the depth of my failure. Among my family — wife bitter, son hurt, my mother despairing — him alone I've managed to make happy.

Just one box to go. Its pairs of cheap cloth gloves, brown lined with red, are stapled together at the heels like loose-hinged shells, time reduced now to these gloves, this dust, this listing sun — the drudgery of menial work. A printer's error, the product labels are badly smudged. . . . No, I can't read it. (Does it mean, Mr. Bob, that they won't let me see him?) My eyes slide faster and faster down the page only to freeze and then lock with a grim fascination, as if spotting my own name among the gravestone rows when driving through a cemetery, on one brief phrase which keeps appearing. In the law's obtuse and antiseptic style, I stand accused, my stay here reduced to a "willful desertion of domicile."

The gloves, the dust, the listing sun. The drudgery of menial work. Day after day without complaint, my father would sort the mail and then walk his route. "You'll turn out just like him," my mother used to say in times of despair, sensing then, through a kind of visionary pessimism, that I too would fail to achieve the sort of career prestige she thought necessary for a man's success. In my son, though, she's found another chance. Allied with my in-laws, she's arisen from her grief and plots again. Expensive clothes, "educational" toys, plans already for private schools (it's the fate of children to be trapped in the current of another generation's unredeemed hopes): with my father dead, I had to resist them alone. A resistance which, I'm ashamed to admit, has ended now.

A bell rings at the front of the store. Still lost in memories, I turn abruptly, but mine is not the son who is

100

passing through the door—I'm greeted instead by the dark green eyes and cropped red hair, by the eerily redundant face, of the Chapman boy. He's prompt, prompt again, another day's labor brought to an end, his presence releasing an habitual sequence, my rotely enacted ritual of leaving. I wave, I nod, I put down the box; I align the last row of gloves and begin to walk — but the direction I take is not toward the door. My legs, it seems, have a will of their own. My legs are leading me step by step, as the sun dips toward the hills and the mill whistle blows and the dust-dotted light sifts among the shelves, to the one place here where I'm frightened to go. Down aisle three. Between the dry goods and the fishing gear. Turning left at the rear of the store. Past the ice cream, the meats, the baskets of produce, the open bin of dairy products. With each step, as if it were a patch of artificial skin sewn to my chest, I can feel the letter tucked in my shirt's breast pocket.

The liquor alcove is small, a kitchen pantry without a door. There, back to me, with hands on his hips and boxes strewn about his feet, my inscrutable boss stares at the shelves. He's so rapt then, so silent, so apparently lost in a serene contemplation of potential profits, that my presence seems a sacrilege, my imminent request the rudest violation of his privacy; and so I freeze, cowed, careful not to move or make a sound, keeping my urgent fears to myself. (*Does it mean, Mr. Bob, that they won't let me see him?*) And yet he knows, somehow he knows.

"Problem?" he asks, still staring at the shelves. When I fail to answer, he slowly turns. He turns, stares, measures, waits; and it seems to me then that the whole mystery of Time and Parenthood has been encoded in his stark, arresting, stonecast face. The same cropped red hair, the same

101

narrow chin and dark green eyes: it's as if I've spanned thirty years in thirty seconds' time, the teenage boy I left behind abruptly aged.

"Nothing — really. It's nothing," I say, mumbling, composure crumbling, turning away; like a lab rat trained to just one route through its maze, I circle back the way I came. The milk, the meat, the baskets of produce; the letter stiff in my shirt's breast pocket. Dust floating up the columns of sunlight. It seems that I don't want his answer, after all, that I want to avoid it. It seems that I've known all along how he would respond; known which of his sayings he'd be bound to select, a perfect fit, words that would lock like Puritan stocks about my wrist.

I hurry down the aisle. Behind me, back to work already, I can hear Mr. Bob adding to the shelves: bottle against bottle, the bell-like rattle, the accidental music of gin, whiskey, muscatel. The Yankee Trader believes, as surely as he believes that Maine is "God's country," in the ethic of self-sufficiency; he believes in each man's right to earn his own way to hell.

Chapman's Yankee Trader, Rte. 45. Clothes, foodstuffs, sandwiches. Candy, in bags hung from hooks like meat left to cure, from the register. Can openers, magnets, the Portland papers; an eye-blurring miscellany of practical products. Everything from *a* to *z*, from Bibles to beer — everything for a price. And everything converging as I rush by, a crush of objects in the narrow aisles, the newspapers fluttering their knee-jerk goodbyes. Calvin Wynn, scarcely animate, acknowledges my departure with a parsimonious dip of his unlit, lip-damp, bummed Lucky Strike. Words are dear. He won't waste them on me, waiting instead for some real folks to arrive.

I burst outside. The cool air, the open lot, a carless stretch of highway — the river beyond. On every shadeless surface, the liquid gilding glint of the low-angled sun. Behind me, its sleigh bells ringing, the store's heavy, spring-loaded door slams shut. Ahead, my tiny Datsun, alone and forlorn on the gravel-strewn lot, seems dwarfed, mocked, like an orphaned fawn, by the enormity of the environment. What precisely do I fear here? The lack of buildings, borders? The chaotic, rotting, softwood forests? The way that even the fairest fall days appear to carry a warning — a quality of unease which, coursing every-where, touching everything, spreads like the first dank breeze of approaching weather? . . . Marjorie's lawyer has sent me a letter.

I quickly cross the lot. Already, to the east, I've seen the first battered pickup truck, point man for the day shift crowd, making its approach down Rte. 45. Husbands, fa-thers, reliable providers — natives of the land. Laughing at jokes I don't understand. One of them, pausing kindly according to custom, will offer Calvin Wynn a match. A story will result, memories of the mill, a mythologizing of the work they share between violent coughs and bursts of smoke. Turning then, bags of candy in their hands, they'll smile to themselves, relieved to see that it's the Chapman boy, one of their own, who'll cash their checks . . .

I turn the key, step on the gas. The Datsun, resisting my panic, surges belatedly across the highway and onto the road to Robin's Nest. I don't look back. I drive too fast: on the edge of the shoulder, jolted by potholes, skimming over the bodies of flattened squirrels, through a blinding brocade of sunlight and shadows, south along the pond toward my dubious shelter . . . my summer nest. There's just a smudge

103

of a line dividing the road. The air through the vent seems unnaturally cold. The truth is that I don't want to see them either, those starveling mill hands, those sons of the fathers my father once knew. Their mute endurance, their day-by-day surrender to duty, has become a reproach. And even their homes, spread along the road — these old frame houses and block-set trailers, surrounded by gardens, spare truck parts, and wood piles grown mountainous through the diligent summer — rebuke me now. Their readiness warns. Their dogs, unchained, bark at my car. Like angry psalms from the self-sufficient God, they seem to prophesy a punishment for all the things I have not done, my failure to prepare for the trial to come.

No garden, no coat, no practical car; not a half a cord of wood left in the shed: winter will arrive and I'll freeze to death. Drop like a bird who's left too late. Burned by the frost like the flowers I've placed on my father's grave. The truth is . . . the truth is that I've known all along what the letter must say. It means, Mr. Bob, that they're locking me out. It means that my stay here, like my mother's stay in her "starter" house, like my father's retreat into his silent self, had become less a phase than a fate — the destiny of guilt.

Another day. Another day, another day. More leaves falling, more dogs barking their angry warnings. The winter will come and I'll still be waiting — without a coat, without a practical car, with my woodstove cold and a colder heart. The winter will come, Mr. Bob, it will come; and I know, as surely as I know the father of the woman I used to love, that they won't permit me to see my son — my dear, dear son . . .

. . . Dear Son: Time, like your father, is running out. This letter, like its author, keeps circling, circling, searching for itself. I wanted to track down and record the world's missing score, find the music within the noise. I wanted to rescue from the chaos of the forest's rotting floor an armored seed, its hardest living core, that irreducible fact which, even if it were sad like my father's eyes, would allow us to live without lying to ourselves, without having to pretend. Let us face each day, and another and another, exactly as it is.

But now, Rob, that search may be coming to an end. For ever since the lawyer's letter arrived, I've been forced to admit that, unlike Calvin Wynn's, mine is not a captive audience; that the season of letters, like the season of apples or lettuce, may be limited; that as the northern snow begins to fall the trail between us just might become impassable. My legal position, I suspect, is not good. My moral standing, I know is worse. My outline's not nearly done, and I'll have no chance to polish what's to come. A.2., A.1., . . . A.3. is next. I'll explain what I can, Rob. In the time that's left, I promise I'll persist.

Your Mother: . . . *we met on campus. Her beauty then was a form of commotion; no still serene profile seen at twilight but a dance at dawn, joyous motion. She seemed so free then, so wondrously free. Like those first exploratory rockets arching past the stratosphere, she had a few brief years at the peak of her life's parabolic curve when she floated, weightless, just beyond the pull of her disapproving family, only then to lose momentum, to drift, fall back in a blaze of sparks and indignant curses, her rebellion extinguished in the deadening brine, the implacable ocean, of her father's cold acquisitive motives. She changed, Rob; she denied, betrayed her* — (careful here) . . . *We met on cam-*

pus. She was uncontainable then, so alive, so urgent; she seemed to radiate concern for other people. She's a wonderful woman, Rob, and will always love you as her son, but she appeared to shift . . . I mean, her eyes acquired an icy tint . . . our thighs, you see, went rigid when they touched — (careful here!) *. . . Your mother, Rob, she . . .*

God: *. . . everyone's hope, obscurely defined. A presence which, while reputed to be everywhere, nevertheless seems impossible to find. Even the predesignated places — icon corners, stony caverns pricked with crosses — are but a priest's wild guess, a specious locus. The church I attended as a boy, for example, hadn't the faintest tinge of holiness. There was among the pews, the railing and the robes, no sense of mystery, no rough-edged longing, no baffled passion for the unseen, self-obliterating forces. The men and women, so carefully dressed, seemed to bow instead to their own decorum.*

In college I deserted God for the Brotherhood of Man. This was the conversion which would soon give birth to the "cherry" civil servant, the dedicated Deputy Inspector of Housing — a commitment I in no way regret. But as theology it proved inadequate: a hug against a hurricane; holding hands before the tidal wave of death. It would be better, Rob, more honest, I think, if God weren't given a name, if we used instead a _____ on the page — silence, empty space, a franker approximation of the demands of faith. On the other hand, I have to confess that religion seems somehow more possible in Maine. I don't know why it is, but the further I am from the world of men, the more I believe that God exists. Once, as the summer passed here, I even tried to pray. I would leave you that at least — the means, the words, a supplicant's access to the divinely obscure, but now as then, when I knelt on the floor of my screened-in porch, I don't know what to say. This letter, it seems, like the life I lead, is still one step removed. A prayer for a prayer. A search for a voice to search for ____ *...*

Sex: *... you will want it; you will need it; It will cause you much joy, confusion, misery. It will occupy, like a rhythmic tide, the harbor of your fantasies. (A tip, Rob: technique is not the most important thing.) Even if all goes well and you overcome the inevitable self-doubts and you find a woman you like and love and want all at once, there will remain, I'm afraid, a final frustration, a wordless despair, a taste of ash in the sweetest sensations. What I mean is ... an estrangement. (Is that what I mean?) Or a sadness maybe, the body humming its own nostalgia. What I mean is this (is this what I mean?): don't be surprised, don't blame yourself, Rob, in the middle of the night, if even satisfaction turns out to be a form of exaction, the very means by which you feel incomplete. (Does that make sense? Will he know what I mean?)*

Maybe I'm wrong. Maybe there's something I've failed to learn: an emotion, a motion, some textbook technique. On the other hand, it doesn't seem ...

Money: *... money is a disease. Your grandfather has been terminally ill for fifty years. Missionary about the plague he carries, he wants to spread the contagion of his unhappiness; wants to tempt, to bribe, to contaminate more innocent lives, and then, when he succeeds, to an-nounce to the world,* I told you so: no one's really different from me. *And yet, to be fair, even the death-grip he applies to your mother's life is an expression of his love — a per-verted hug, a desperate caring. It's just these sorts of paradoxes that a letter like this ought to be explaining ...*

107

Death: . . . *the unimaginable, the unmentionable; avoidance of the topic is the greatest of all the many lies we tell. And our lying in turn becomes an ally of death; we allow and encourage what we refuse to admit. In World War II, for example, Rob, the Nazis killed six million Jews; they wholesaled death, they warehoused it, a fact so monstrous that we prefer to disarm it by quibbling about its mathematics. Specious evasions. Scholarly debates as to whether accounts were "exaggerated."*

Accounts are not exaggerated, Rob. "It" — the unimaginable, the unmentionable — happens to us all, a conclusion you'd find hard to draw while living in a town like Colton Falls whose central purpose behind its schools and yards, whose secret psychological cause, is to limit your chances of seeing a corpse. Here by contrast bodies abound. Fallen tree trunks, shells of insects, bits of bird skull, the eyeless rotting hides of squirrels — there are times, leaden-sky days, winter descending like a shadow from the north, when this entire sandy landscape, beach and pond and hills and farms, seem on the verge of becoming a corpse. My father became a corpse while reading in his chair. My mother confided to me later that although he often fell asleep over a book, there was a quality to his stillness, an unspecifiable difference, which told her right away. I wondered, but didn't ask, if what had prompted her to look then was his failure to answer when she called his name. I still can hear her call his name . . .

I don't want you, Rob, to be afraid. (Is that at all possible when I am so afraid?) I want somehow to keep you safe, both to shelter you and to tell the truth, to encourage you even as I let you know that the Nazis killed . . . that the people you love, that you yourself . . . Here, then gone;

108

here, then gone. *I can't lie to you, Rob: the unmentionable happens, happens to us all. Even worse perhaps, what exactly happens when it happens (at least to me) remains unclear, obscure like God. I don't want you to be afraid, but all I have is guesses. I know the facts but not their lesson. Death has come to seem, the longer I've looked, less like a concept than a species of conjecture — a perpetual, personal one-word question. To which, I'm afraid, I have no answer.*

But then you've heard that before — haven't you, Rob? Like the crow with its idiotic caw, *I seem to have, whatever the topic at hand, the same dumbly erumpent, dispiriting response.* I-don't-know, I-don't-know, I-don't-know, I-don't-know, *I keep squawking from my perch at the world below. And yet if this letter's to be honest. I don't know how else I'm supposed to . . .*

This is it? *This* is it — the letter that was meant to do much, my special gift? It was supposed to be your wood pile, your jacket, your sensible blanket, some insurance against the inevitable winter. It was supposed to make you self-sufficient — wise in my absence. I write and I write, I wait and I wait. My words streak haphazardly down the page, as uncontrollable as rain. Like my father in his shop, I murmur to my thoughts, "Fit now," "Don't split on me"; like him, I want to fashion for you a model world, a finer world, and yet no matter how many drafts I do, I seem to lack the necessary blend of character and skill to transcend my mean materials. What I've written, what I've made — I'm forced to conclude, Rob, after all these pages — is no better than myself. The same confusion exists, the ambivalence; the same knotted web of love, panic, incompetence. The letter, like my life, is a rampant mess. To read it is to see again, in all its stupefying incoherence, the Chief Inspector's lunchtime desk.

And now, Rob, there's no time left; no chance to cross out and start again. October's here. October, with its dead leaves and legalities, its impoverished text. A world being stripped of adjectives. October's here and A.5., the standard sign-off, the absent father's parting line, is scheduled next — "in an upbeat mood," the letter's death. But . . . but if . . .

I came here in July, Rob, I came in July. To Robin's Nest. In the wake of my grief. Dock, canoe, child-safe beach. There were moments at the start, whole days carried high on the wave of my escape, when I seemed on the verge of some transfiguring peace. But my words have betrayed me. My letter, I can't help feeling, has failed to capture how close I came, the progress I've made; it's failed to describe the weight of the days here, their gathering momentum, never quite conveying the minute exactions of exile's boredom, its erosion of pretense, how the grit of slow time abrades the mind, how the landscape of self is made to change when merging with a beach in mid-July: sparrows chirping, a robin hopping, ants and sand and the waves' *slap-slap,* the acrobatic sex of dragonflies. A heron emerging (you should have seen it, Rob — a miraculous occurrence); a heron emerging, perfect in its flight. I came in July. I risked everything, my heart's last hold on the hope of a home, by leaving you behind. It's true, I confess, what the lawyer said. I *am* a willful deserter of domicile, I *did* choose what I did, choose to run out, and I know that this might seem just a cowardly attempt to justify myself. But the fog's begun to clear, Rob, it has begun to clear. I really have caught glimpses of that tapestry of truth whose description was to be my legacy to you. The strands are all here — the heron in the pond; the mother, father, and only son; the Chief Inspector's PLAN AHEa_d sign; Helene, Calvin Wynn, and Mr. Bob — if I could just weave them together, rearrange the letter; if I could just present to you in words what I believe that I've heard, the music within the world's rude noise: life and death, life and death, a minnow, shiny as tin, swallowed whole by another fish who is swallowed whole by another fish, who are all part of the same event, neither more nor less, the same errorless dance moving to the beat of life's austere arithmetic; predator and prey, punch-clock days, men becoming corpses sitting in their chairs, here, then gone/here, then gone, first class, second class, each letter, each body to its appropriate box, twenty-five cents for a lollipop, so many men working so many hours for so much pay submitting to their duty in pickup trucks . . .

(This is it? *This* is it — the letter meant to be my legacy, my one lasting gift? It was supposed to be like the owner's directions. It was supposed to guide you, clearly, firmly, to your destination; to warn of wrong turns, to point out the signs, adding if it could, in a lightning storm of exclamation points, a parenthetical list of recommended sights: ["Take a walk on a clear summer night and stare up at the stars!"] ["Watch the slow unfolding of a water lily blossom in the soft silver light of an August dawn!"] It was supposed to be your compass, Rob . . . your street guide, your star chart . . . your map through life.)

I came here in July. A willful deserter nestled among the pines. I came alone, without money, without clothes; I came to grieve for my father and to rescue myself — I left

111

you behind. The Yankee Trader's right: everything, it seems, every choice we make, no matter how obscure, has its preordained price. We're billed for what we do; I chose what I chose and alternatives exclude. A finite man, there's no way, Rob, that I could have both come to Maine and have stayed with you. Three months have now passed, a million moments gone that we might have shared, a million chances lost, and I'm reminded each day by the absence of your face that in searching for my father I've neglected my son.

Are you all right? Can you understand at all why I've done what I've done — what, whom, I came here to find? My words, I'm afraid, have betrayed me. My letter, I can't help but feel, has failed to capture that missing mailman, the power of his presence, how his silence was the silence of the inwardly strong, with the aura of a vocation like that of a monk's — the moral courage of abstinence; it's failed to convey his strange composure, that palpable calm which seemed to promise always that he knew something more, which made the long-winded explanations of others seem nervous and insecure, which made them, his supposed betters (Uncle Teddy, for example, and his executive friends), turn to him as my mother did, his name on their lips, wanting somehow to be confirmed. I've given you the sadness but not the peace. I've captured the superficial surrender but not the undeceived tranquility — his unique capacity to accept the truth. It was as if he always carried his workshop with him, his own special room; it was as if he were never far from his own Maine pond, a still private place from which he could observe, without fear of becoming lost, each moment in his life exactly as it was. What must it be like to have such a place, a moral base, a geography to enclose one's soul? What must it be like, day after day, to live with the truth?

I don't know . . . *I-don't-know, I-don't-know, I-don't-know, I-don't-know*. I write and I write, I wait and I wait. My words streak haphazardly down the page. Positioned on my porch, I sit and rock, sit and watch, the dying day's light shimmering on the pond, the endless letter lying on my lap. All around me, a silence seems to fall like a windless snow. I can almost feel the tree shadows stretching, their long fingers of darkness slowly interlacing, my own pale fingers stiffening in the cold. Minutes pass. A wind begins to blow. Flexing my hands, I try to warm them with my breath, but I won't go in, won't move from where I am, afraid to drop my pen, to end. Afraid to fail.

I want to give you something more. There ought to be a way, before I sign my name, before A.5. is entered on the page, to sum up the subtle secrets that I've learned; there ought to be a way to say what my father would have said, in that nonexistent second letter of his, if he had been a man of words. Something wise, something brief. Not *the* answer but *an* answer, a practical tip. A sign, if not a map, pointing the way out. A terse word-arrow drawn as if from the aphoristic quiver of Mr. Bob and guaranteed to strike the truth. If we are not what we own, as people want to believe in Colton Falls, and we are not who we control, as people like to think at City Hall — who are we then? What *does* it mean to be a man?

Robin's Nest, two miles south of Rte. 45. The damp sand . . . the branches' dark web . . . the network of shadows closing on the ground . . . the way the last light pools, like liquefied gold, on the surface of the pond, a glistening base for the dying weeds and skeletal trees on the shore be-

113

yond— I wish you could see it, Rob: my inlet, before sunset, resolving into fall. Day by day, as the summer's extravagant decor has drifted away, this wedge of open space, this glimpse from the sill of my rented nest, has deepened, widened. The longer I've stayed, the further I've penetrated into the realm of the northern horizon. Beyond the bog, the sand, through bared birch stands, past the mill stacks and steeples, past barn-board sheds on rocky hillocks, dissolving in a blur of farms and forest—soon, if more shades of opacity can be stripped away, I'll see all the way to Little Chester.

Loneliness, it seems, if suffered patiently, can become a kind of clarity. In time, you see more; you begin to see what has always been there behind the foliage of deceit, those lies we tell to decorate the void. It's occurred to me now as I sit and rock, sit and watch, that I've known the missing answer all along. It's occurred to me now that, like the cottage across the pond which I failed to spot until the leaves were down, my father's advice has always been close, the inlet's ghost, an implicit truth waiting to be voiced. To find it has been a matter of patience, of silence, of letting passing things pass and the stillness ripen until the landscape assumes the precise weight and shape of an irreducible emotion, until setting mirrors self and self setting, and you know what must be known and the wind becomes your voice and the pen begins to move with a will of its own as you sit and watch from your screened-in porch, a small globe of light in the descending dark.

No, we are not what we own. No, we are not who we control. My father would have said, his whole life implied, that men and women should be judged by the higher standards of the artisan, by the care they've taken with the

114

work they've done. He would have said, Rob, if forced to speak at all, that we are how we do our jobs. Craftsman to wood. Mailman to route. Husband to wife. Father to son.

Here it is then — at last a useful aphorism. I wanted to give you more but my letter's a mess and I've rescued this at least, one nugget of truth from my slag pile of words: *you are how you do your job*. Always remember that, Rob. And now I'm supposed to conclude (in an upbeat mood, as reassuring as possible), and now I'm supposed to say to you, as a father to his son . . .

. . . The word *son* — I never much liked it as a term of address when I was growing up. On the lips of certain friends' fathers, split-level tyrants, the kind given to barking out orders from sports field sidelines, it was applied like a collar, like the brand of a rancher, less a sign of affection than an insecure man's proclamation of possession. But since you were born, Rob, since I've become a father myself, I find that the word has acquired a new attraction. It seems remade, reshaped, for my own lips and tongue; custom-cut to fit like my father's crafted joints, like the heron to the pond. I want to say it, to hear it; the phrase "Dear Son" when emerging on the page has a touching and irresistible appearance. And the source of its appeal is not self-congratulations. I repeat the word "Son" not to boast of what I own but to wonder at the strangeness and strength of what I feel: this affinity of selves; this immeasurable, irreducible, indescribable bond. The most important sensations are the hardest to explain — how it feels to stare at a sky struck with stars; the way I felt when I first held you in my arms — experiences so large that *we* inhabit them and not vice versa; so beyond our scope that we are carried in their tide like bits of single-celled life in the swell of the ocean. I love you, Rob, because you are my son. Without knowing you, I loved you; from the first moment I saw you, I loved you; when I'm dead, if it's possible, I'll love you still. I loved your mother once, for reasons perhaps not exactly clear, but reasons nonetheless, reasons which seemed to have disappeared. You are beyond reasons. You I will love as I loved my father, as I love him still; as I love my mother, whom on occasion I don't even like. Because you are you. Because you are my son. And this, I promise you, you can not lose. I will always love you, Rob; I will always love you even though . . .

I came here in July, Rob, I came in July. To Robin's Nest. Dock, canoe, child-safe beach. I came to grieve for my father and to find myself; I left you behind and have no excuse. This letter was meant to take my place; it was intended as a gift, a living lasting legacy in words. But now that summer's passed and illusions have faded and I see myself clearly, the man that I am, in the devolving face of the autumn landscape, I've come to accept that my father's memory is all I possess that's worthy of you. His advice — hypothetical, deduced — is not enough. What you need is his life, that odd but reassuring presence by your side: keys dangling from a bathroom chair, a razor poised in surgical hands, a gentle reveille of knocks easing you awake day after day. What you need is what I received: not letters but actions, a legacy of example — memory upon memory, like a stream in a canyon, etching over time an enduring pattern. For as the fog begins to clear and my confusion gives way in evaporating shades to a grief as pure as the mountain air, I begin to understand, shamefully late, that I *was* given those answers I thought I was missing, that my father, in fact, lived them, that the second letter which I wanted so badly was written each day in the bold and legible script of his behavior.

But that script is now gone — here, then gone; my father's dead and all that I've offered in his place is a scattershot spray of belated words. My father's dead, my summer of exile come to an end, and all I have left, my only justification for refusing to quit, is the need I feel now to honor, to thank him, to do justice to his memory. The obligation I feel to try one last time to inscribe for you an epitaph for the missing mailman.

You should have known him, Rob. He was like the land to which he was born: silent, self-sufficient, honest, and strong. He met his own standards — as a craftsman, as a father. He did his job.

My mother was wrong. I haven't turned out like Dad, not yet anyway. Even though I've come to the land to which he was born; even though I've dropped out, too, "under-achiever" still printed on my card. I don't have that small serene room sequestered inside, that self-centering pond. I haven't met his high standards, I'm not one of life's crafts-men; now more than ever, I could not pass his stare's inspection: . . . I haven't done my job. The minimum wage a father must pay is not, after all, an apology — it's being there. Moment by moment, day after day, being there. And I am gone.

Robin's Nest, two miles south of Rte. 45. Damp sand. The branches' dark web. The network of shadows closing on the ground. On every surface, threads connect, patterns filling in as possibilities are shed: past becoming present, life becoming death, sons becoming fathers, more letters to be written, formal notes to lawyers pleading for forgiveness . . . Inevitably night comes, closing us in, dimming what

117

might have been with the ever finer mesh of the things we've done.

It won't be long now. Earth and water merge, pond with shore, the stripped nerves of the trees slowly being sheathed by the darkening sky. It won't be long now. October too will fade, more superfluous adjectives ripped away, the long Maine winter soon to arrive. I can already feel it sifting through the screen, that cold slow breath of December's sleep; I can already feel it in the stiffening of my fingers — the dullness, the hardness, the intravenous darkness of a comatose land. (Can I survive till spring? Will I awake in May a better man?) I know that it's late, I know that I chose what I chose and alternatives exclude and that words alone cannot reassure but I promise, I do promise that I'll come to you soon — if they let me, if I can.

In the meantime, I wait. I write and I wait, my fingers growing cold, my pen slowing down, less and less room, nearer, always nearer to the bottom of the page. I wait for permission, for an answer. I wait for a visitation from Little Chester. I wait — a father and a son; a pilgrim out of place — for genealogy and geography to work their magic.

The inlet grows still, so still. The cottage is being swallowed by the shadow of the hills, the reflected sun, a dull gold smudge, sinking like a coin thrown for good luck into the marshy murk of the pond. Not a sound to be heard, not a movement. Birdless, windless, leafless, wordless . . . somewhere — not here — some mill hand's home, tired heads bowed over hard-earned food, they'll be offering a prayer of thanks to Jesus. No, it won't be long now: the last touch of sun wrung from the air; the pen drawn down to its own horizon, nearer, always nearer to the bottom of the page. I sit and rock, sit and watch, afraid to go in, to end — afraid to say what I must say.

I will always love you, Rob; I will always love you even though . . . even though I might not be there.

This is it, then, this *is* it — the outline finished, the letter ended; no more apologies, advice, confused reminiscence. At last, the last memo from the desk of the willfully deserting Deputy Inspector. All that's left, the only P.S., is to choose the wrapping, the envelope for this meager package.

I'm sending you the best. My letter will arrive, first class, folded within the velvet chamber of a tiny wooden treasure chest; it will come enclosed in a handmade miniature music box, with leather strap hinges and seamless corners and antique filigreed gold lock and key, and with a mechanical voice programmed to sing, upon the raising of its lid, the soothing notes of a Brahms' serenade. Tend to it well, this specially selected envelope. It's the one object in my life I care about, the one thing I own which transcends its mean materials. Feel its surface, its fine edges; admire its workmanship with your eyes, your mind, your fingertips — study it as I've studied my inlet. Sense, if you can, how it was joined, with what precision and care, the effort expended, the love and commitment, the intricate weave of qualities, that fingerprint of character, which has been left behind by the box's maker: there's a lesson there. And when you raise the domed lid and the music emerges and you find yourself moved by the slow unfolding of its gentle phrases, please don't think of me as I was, fighting with your mother in Colton Falls, or even try to imagine me as I might become, chastened by a winter in Johnson Mills. Instead, imagine if you can, while picturing the virtuoso dance of the maker's working hands, a man's baritone voice, a voice in song, fixing not on the lyrics it shapes or

119

the tune it traces but on the voice itself, its signature in sound, how it rises and falls with an unself-conscious confidence, a message within the world's raw noise. Imagine that message is meant for you. Imagine awaking to that voice, awash in its warmth, how it seeps into your room through the veins of the house, how it enwraps, enfolds, encloses you, and how it then floats, a world of its own in the void of the dark, carrying you within its peaceful globe, far above the phantom fears of night, safe until the daylight comes . . .

That, I'm afraid, is the best I can do. I don't know about God, about women, about sex and death — not nearly enough. I haven't found among the bullshit memos and sunstruck ponds, the scripted mornings and herons in flight — among the whole confusing collage of the absurd and the sacred which has been my life — an outline of answers, an infallible list of aphorisms. All I have instead is what I've been given. All I have is a soul's song in wood, a model shaped by another man's wisdom. So take the box and this sorry letter, and if by some miracle they work together and you get the feeling I want you to, the same sense of safety which I used to feel when hearing my father through my bedside grill, then know who it is who deserves your thanks, know whose voice is the one which reassures.

Because it's from him, you see; the gift's really from him. Because he *was* there on that winter morning and every other morning, year after year — the mailman on his route, the music box-maker poised above his wood. Because I can't sing the way my father could.